Donald MacKenzie and The Murder Room

》》 This title is part of The Murder Room, our series dedicated to making available out-of-print or hard-to-find titles by classic crime writers.

Crime fiction has always held up a mirror to society. The Victorians were fascinated by sensational murder and the emerging science of detection; now we are obsessed with the forensic detail of violent death. And no other genre has so captivated and enthralled readers.

Vast troves of classic crime writing have for a long time been unavailable to all but the most dedicated frequenters of second-hand bookshops. The advent of digital publishing means that we are now able to bring you the backlists of a huge range of titles by classic and contemporary crime writers, some of which have been out of print for decades.

From the genteel amateur private eyes of the Golden Age and the femmes fatales of pulp fiction, to the morally ambiguous hard-boiled detectives of mid twentieth-century America and their descendants who walk our twenty-first century streets, The Murder Room has it all. **》》**

The Murder Room
Where Criminal Minds Meet

themurderroom.com

T0352173

Donald MacKenzie 1908–1994

Donald MacKenzie was born in Ontario, Canada, and educated in England, Canada and Switzerland. For twenty-five years MacKenzie lived by crime in many countries. 'I went to jail,' he wrote, 'if not with depressing regularity, too often for my liking.' His last sentences were five years in the United States and three years in England, running consecutively. He began writing and selling stories when in American jail. 'I try to do exactly as I like as often as possible and I don't think I'm either psychopathic, a wayward boy, a problem of our time, a charming rogue. Or ever was.'

He had a wife, Estrela, and a daughter, and they divided their time between England, Portugal, Spain and Austria.

Raven and the Kamikaze

Donald MacKenzie

An Orion book

Copyright © The Estate of Donald MacKenzie 1977

The right of Donald MacKenzie to be identified as the author of this work has
been asserted in accordance with the Copyright, Designs and Patents Act 1988.

This edition published by
The Orion Publishing Group Ltd
Orion House
5 Upper St Martin's Lane
London WC2H 9EA

An Hachette UK company
A CIP catalogue record for this book is available from the British Library

ISBN 978 1 4719 0501 8

www.orionbooks.co.uk

To the memory of the original London Zilch Club:
Cap, Clare and Jojo, Christophe, Sug the Hug and the
bold bad Quirk.

CHAPTER ONE

Raven and Zaleski, Tuesday

John Raven was lying flat on his back on the deck of the *Albatross*. His eyes were shut and he dozed like an animal, reassured by the familiar pattern of sounds. The bump of the houseboat against the heavy tyres that served as fenders, the drone of distant traffic, the raucous cries of the gulls overhead. It was evening but the heat of the day lingered on. A haze hung over the river and the gnats were biting.

A new noise invaded his consciousness, the repetitive ringing of his telephone. He hauled himself up and padded barefoot across the deck in candy-striped shorts. The door to the big room was open. Summer light brightened the colours of the Klee hanging on the end wall. The shabby leather sofa was hot from the sun and he sat down gingerly. He picked up the 'phone. He'd long since given up announcing his name or number. Those who mattered would know.

'Yes?'

His caller identified himself. 'Casimir Zaleski.'

Raven scratched at a bony brown shoulder. 'Casimir Zaleski. Well now, it's been a long time, Casimir.'

'How are you?' the voice inquired solicitously. 'How are you, my friend?'

'Fine,' said Raven, his face thoughtful. 'How about you?'

'Good,' said Zaleski. 'So why never coming to see me?'

Raven scratched his gnat-bites, pondering the question. It must be all of three years since he'd heard the rasping accent. The voice had lost none of its confidence.

'I didn't know I'd been invited,' Raven said mildly.

Zaleski sounded shocked. 'Invited! Old friends are needing invitations? Come on, now!'

Raven lit a cigarette. The skin on his right wrist where he wore his watch was pale.

'Old friends?' he queried.

'Comrades,' Zaleski amended. 'People are telling me Raven this, Raven that. No longer inspector-detective, they say. But from my comrade I hear nothing.'

Raven flicked ash at the carpet. Sunlight searched out the darns and mends in the faded Aubusson.

'You've got it all wrong, Casimir. I think about you constantly. You're not speaking from jail by any chance?'

Zaleski laughed like a man who has just been stepped on by a superior.

'Jokes from bloody policeman! Now listen, mate. Why not having dinner with me in *Wielkapolska*?'

Raven's mind leaped back into the dark airless restaurant, recalling the succession of herring dishes, pickled tongue with raisin sauce, the odour of sour beet juice.

'I'll tell you,' he said, combing fingers through long brown-grey hair. 'I don't go out much these days.'

Zaleski hurdled the suggestion easily. 'But to *Wielka-polska*! You'll see – everything is changed, mate. Over two thousand pounds for curtains and carpets. New chef, French bastard. People are coming from high and wide to eat. I am losing bloody voice saying hello, goodbye, thank you. You'll come tonight and we'll talk of old times. Nine o'clock, O.K.?'

Raven fitted a face to the voice, seeing the high cheekbones protecting deepset eyes, prominent nose and smiling mouth. There was something indomitable about the image, a romantic refusal to accept the reality of failure. Whatever else, Zaleski was good value.

'What's the time now?' Raven asked indulgently. His watch was in the bedroom and the grandfather clock had never adjusted to the movement of the boat on the river.

'It is precisely,' Zaleski repeated the word with pleasure. 'Precisely twenty minutes past seven.'

'Nine o'clock,' promised Raven and put the 'phone down. His towel was still on deck. He went outside, a tall narrow-shouldered man with the last of the sun on his back.

Other craft were moored on both sides of *Albatross*, most of them connected by ramshackle catwalks. The river-steamer converted to restaurant anchored a couple of hundred yards downstream was a new venture. Diners reached it by launch. There was little noise and only occasionally a smell of cooking from the kitchen. Raven hauled in his dinghy and took out the oars. He stood for a while, staring at the darting fish he never seemed able to catch. Living on the converted barge had given him a sense of peace he had found nowhere else. He enjoyed the city without being part of it. He watered the hydrangeas wired to the bulwarks, took the last of the beef-stew from the refrigerator and threw it over the side.

His trust fund was invested in stocks and something he didn't profess to understand had happened the previous January. The result was a windfall of three thousand pounds, tax paid. A girl he knew in the interior-decorating business had talked him into having his bedroom done over. The job had only just been finished and he still wasn't sure about the french-grey and charcoal walls,

3

basketwork bed and patterned venetian blinds. The one certain advantage was the step-in wardrobe that covered one entire wall. It was made of untreated cedar and imparted a faintly exotic aroma to his clothes. His bathroom windows overlooked the stern of the neighbouring boat. He could see its owner on deck, clad in a loincloth, facing the waning sun, his greenbearded head bent in apparent meditation. The Great Dane lying beside him was gently snoring.

Raven showered and wondered what he should wear. Remembering Zaleski's elegance, he felt that his usual costume of jeans, shirt and sneakers lacked the style the Pole might expect. As a cop Raven had been given to velvet. He chose cream-coloured slacks, a rust silk shirt and brown-and-white shoes. He unlocked the Jacobean desk that had been his grandmother's and took twenty pounds from the secret drawer. Zaleski was given to sudden surprises when it came to money.

The intervening years had gone quickly. It had been Raven's last case. A jewelled monstrance had been stolen while on exhibition. The circumstances were peculiar. The monstrance was technically on loan from the Italian government and the incident was on its way to creating a diplomatic squabble. Raven had broken the case in his own unorthodox manner, finding the prime culprits to be three middle-aged and raffish Poles of whom Zaleski was one. Stage two of the robbery involved a notoriously unloved thug that the Yard had been chasing for years. Circumstances and a liking for Zaleski had allowed Raven to let the Poles off the hook, concentrating on the professional villain. Zaleski appeared on television in the guise of public hero, accepting a cash award from a national newspaper as no more than his natural due. It was the last Raven had seen of him.

It was eight-thirty when he locked both doors, one leading out on deck, the other at the embankment end of the gangway. An overhead garland of rusted barbed-wire discouraged the antics of local boy-burglars. He crossed the street, glancing by habit up the alley where his car was parked. His greenbearded neighbour owned the Herbarium and parking rights.

The Citroën's new spring paint job glistened back reassuringly. He walked north as far as Kings Road, exchanging smiles with the one-eyed newspaper-vendor and the girl who worked at Dapper Dan's Dyers and Cleaners. It was days like this, he thought, that made England just about the best place in the world to live. It was the country not the people. Otherwise he'd have taken off for the Azores or somewhere and thought about the book he would never write. He took his time, enjoying the mass of roses near the Chelsea Arts Club, the barelegged girls who hurried past smelling of scent and confident in crisp cotton dresses.

His choice of direction took him past a small block of redbrick flats facing east. He turned into the forecourt on impulse and scanned the list of occupants underneath the voice-box. A visiting-card identified the resident in apartment 1 as *CASIMIR ZALESKI, Count of the Holy Roman Empire*. The pencilled scribble on the card had been partially erased but was still legible:

in pub, Back in halfanhour or theirabout.

Zaleski's curtains were drawn, blocking the view of the curious.

A noise turned Raven's head. A tall girl emerged from the entrance dressed in a sleeveless brown linen frock. Her skin was splashed with freckles and dark-red hair complemented her green eyes. She rested her weight on one heel, gold hoops swinging from her ears as she looked at Raven curiously.

Raven grinned self-consciously. 'Hello!'

'Hi!' she said easily. 'Is it Casimir you want?'

'Only in a manner of speaking,' he answered. Her accent was North American and she had the self-assurance that went with it.

She frowned slightly. 'Are you a friend of his?'

Raven recognized the note of caution. Obviously she lived in the building.

'I'm having dinner with him.'

Her face cleared. 'Then you want the restaurant. Do you know where it is?'

He moved away from the curtained windows. 'I know.'

He held the small iron gate open for her. She went through, wafting *Calèche*, and then stopped.

'Thank you. Did anyone ever tell you that you have a highly irritating manner?'

'Frequently,' Raven admitted. 'I try not to let it discourage me.'

He took his time walking to Fulham Road, trying to think of a single word that would describe Zaleski. 'Rogue' lacked the endearing quality that made people like that girl feel protective towards him. 'Rascal' perhaps came closer. Raven waited at the junction of Fulham Road and Drayton Gardens, recalling the bitter night of three winters before. Television technicians, ashen-faced with cold, huddling in the lee of the sound truck, waiting to connect the power cables. A red-nosed and ear-muffed producer chatting nervously to a couple of uniformed cops while a small crowd stared at the faded curtains behind which Zaleski awaited his hour of triumph. He had entered it drunk, wearing a chaplet of spare-rib grease on his cashmere sweater, and with a bottle of vintage Krug in his hand. Later on he'd sung a couple of arias from Verdi, denounced de Gaulle as a traitor to France and passed out in the ladies' lavatory.

The signals changed. A couple of hundred yards west, Raven stopped, startled by the changed aspect of *Wielkapolska*. The entire front of the restaurant had been repainted in gold and white. Gone the doorway littered with dead leaves, yellowed newspapers and empty milk bottles. The woodwork was stained and varnished. A crowned eagle hung above the entrance. Raven opened the door. The walls were hung with elegant silkworked scarves. A girl in a Polish costume was serving drinks to people at the bar. Raven scanned the crowded room till he found his host at a table near the window. Zaleski rose quickly and hurried forward, both arms outstretched. He was a foot shorter than Raven with the rolling gait of a deep-water sailor. He was wearing a blazer with silver buttons, cream flannel trousers and a scarf decorated with Lipizzaners. He rose on his toes and locked Raven in a close embrace, his hair exuding an aroma of eau-de-Portugal.

'Welcome to *Wielkapolska*!' He stepped back, hanging on to Raven's arm and shaking his head with admiration. 'No different! Not bloody older! Fantastic!'

He led Raven to the window-table and released him reluctantly. They both sat. The bottle of vodka between them had been embedded in a block of ice its own shape. Only the neck was free. Zaleski filled a couple of glasses, his smile displaying new bridgework.

'So, mate,' he said fondly. 'Bloody cheers!'

Raven raised his glass. It was difficult to stop being infected by the other man's artless welcome. He drank the vodka as his host had taught, throwing his head back and emptying the glass at one throw. He covered the glass with his hand as Zaleski tilted the bottle again.

'Let me get my breath first,' he pleaded. The chilled spirit was already making a pool of warmth in his stomach.

Attentive waiters flitted between the candlelit tables. Chopin tinkled from hidden speakers. There was an aura of prosperity, a smell of well-cooked food, expensive perfumes, Turkish cigarettes. Raven looked across the table.

'A change indeed. This is quite a production. How did you manage it?'

Zaleski waved airily. 'Bank is advancing money.'

'The *bank*?' Raven said incredulously. '*Which* bank? You used to have to wear a false nose to get from one end of the street to the other.'

'Everything different now,' Zaleski said behind raised finger. 'Bloody bank manager is finally understanding.' He unbuttoned his blazer releasing a roll of fat above his waist. He patted it, grinning. 'Is muscle.'

Raven groped for a cigarette. 'I passed by your flat. Do you know something, Casimir? I never realized that you were a count. I didn't think they had them in Poland.'

'On my mother's side,' Zaleski explained. 'Is difficult to explain to English people. Don't worry about it.'

He snapped his fingers for a waiter, his sleek black hair shining in the light of the candles. There was no grey in it.

'I have already ordered,' he announced. 'Just eating civilized food. Serve!' he said to the waiter.

He fitted a monocle in the slot of flesh under his right eye and peered round the table at Raven's legs.

'Nice trousers. Very nice. Now you see in Cairo I was having uniforms made of same material.'

Raven winced. It all came back with a rush. Cairo, Jerusalem, staff cars, soldier-servants and the delights of the bazaars. Zaleski's war service was a springboard for memories of a privileged past.

'It's good to see you like this,' Raven said impulsively. 'I'm really impressed.'

'Is luck,' Zaleski said modestly. 'The other two wasted their share of reward. Bloody Poles. Now coming here eating for nothing. How is the beautiful Cathy?'

Raven wiped his mouth carefully. 'She's dead,' he said shortly.

Zaleski's deepset eyes clouded. His voice was suddenly formal. 'Excuse me, mate. I am sorry.'

Raven shrugged. He had learned to live with the memory but to share it was impossible. He drank from his refilled glass.

'And your wife?'

Zaleski's mind was on other matters. 'Hanya is always well. Thank God.'

Raven thought of the general's daughter painting flowers on plates to help pay the debts of a man she no longer lived with.

'Is she still living in the same place?'

Zaleski dislodged a piece of bread from his expensive bridgework. 'I am making provision for Hanya. She reads and sees her friends. Once a month we go to concert. I have given Hanya best years of my life.'

Raven looked up sharply. The Pole's gaze was unblinking. 'That must be something to remember,' Raven said gravely. But as far as Zaleski was concerned the subject was closed.

He talked non-stop for the next three-quarters of an hour, touching on the ingratitude of the British, the fallacy of democracy, a belly dancer he had known in Alexandria.

Raven listened. Peppered steak was served with purple blooms of broccoli and *pommes Lyonnaises*. The Beaujolais was perfect. They were on the coffee when movement caught his eye in the mirror. He glanced across at the entrance. The girl he had seen outside Zaleski's flat had just come in and was going to the bar. Her escort was a thin-faced man with Tartar eyes and short white hair. Zaleski was watching the couple openly, thin-lipped and hostile. He blew the candle out and leaned across the table, beckoning conspiratorially.

'K.G.B.,' he whispered, mouthing each letter distinctly. His eyes flicked sideways indicating the couple at the bar.

Raven blinked. Zaleski had put away five vodkas and his share of the wine and he must have been drinking earlier.

'K.G.B.,' repeated Raven.

Zaleski signalled caution, a nerve pushing under the skin near his nose. He beckoned Raven into closer contact.

'This man sitting at bar. You see?'

Raven had an uncomfortable feeling that he was about to be embarrassed. It was some time since he had read Zaleski's Aliens Office file but certain details were clear in his memory. The Pole had a record of four arrests. Drunk and Disorderly. Drunk and Resisting Arrest. Insulting Behaviour and Disturbing the Peace. On the last occasion he had celebrated the birthday of Kosciusco with friends in a Chelsea wine bar. He left smarting from a deep sense of rejection and harangued a crowd of local football fans who were under the impression that he supported a rival team. Three plate glass windows were smashed. Zaleski was fined £50 and bound over to be of good behaviour.

'I see him,' Raven said shortly.

Zaleski's hooked nose thinned. 'Communist spy. Probably K.G.B.'

'You're drunk,' retorted Raven.

Zaleski shook his head. The man and the girl had moved to a nearby table. The girl's hands were expressive as she made her points.

'You want to listen or not?' demanded Zaleski.

Raven shrugged. 'Do I have any choice?'

Zaleski's voice was urgent. The red-haired girl was Barbara Beattie, a Canadian working in B.B.C. research. She'd first brought her escort to *Wielkapolska* three weeks before. The couple had eaten there half-a-dozen times since. The man was a Pole called Henryk Lamprecht.

Raven looked sideways. The girl was still doing the talking. 'Lamprecht,' said Zaleski significantly. 'Is German descent. Pomeranian. I am spending my summer holidays there.'

Raven nodded. 'So?'

Zaleski looked right and left and worked himself nearer. 'So why mixing Russian with Polish? I have spoken with him. Barbara was introducing.'

'You're smashed,' said Raven. 'Let me take you home.'

The nerve jumped in Zaleski's face. The suggestion seemed to have offended him. He rapped himself in the region of the heart, enunciating with some difficulty.

' "Mr. Zaleski's behaviour exemplary throughout. Worthy of highest traditions of his race." Who is saying that, please?'

Raven shrugged. There were two ways of looking at it. He chose the one that related to the facts.

'A Central Criminal Court judge who didn't know that Mr. Zaleski was a melon-headed windbag who should have been in the dock instead of the witness box. A rascal copping a five-thousand-pound reward for public service. Public *service*!' He shook his head sorrowfully.

He wiped his mouth and folded his napkin. 'Goodnight, Casimir. Thanks for my dinner. My regards to your wife.'

Zaleski's hand shot forward. The grip on Raven's arm was surprisingly powerful.

'You don't want to listen?'

Raven sat down again. 'For crissakes, Casimir. O.K., I'll listen. Just don't expect me to get involved.'

Zaleski took the wraps off his story one by one using some strange and involved Slavic logic. Count one in his indictment was Lamprecht's frequent employment of Russian idioms, count two the fact that Poles in London tended to know one another, by repute if not personally. Nobody had ever heard of Lamprecht, nor did he figure on the registry of ex-servicement kept at the Sikorski Institute. Raven listened with a sense of having been there before. It was after eleven but the restaurant was still doing business. He thought of the new batch of records waiting for him on the houseboat. He hadn't even opened the package. He sneaked another look in the slender gilt-framed mirror. Lamprecht and the girl were completely absorbed in one another's conversation. Barbara Beattie had a trick of flicking her hair back with her hand as she talked.

'O.K.,' Raven said wearily. 'He's a Communist spy and he's watching you. Where's that supposed to get him?'

Zaleski's eyes slitted like blinds. 'You have not heard of Polish government-in-exile?'

12

'But indeed,' said Raven. 'I know the Foreign Minister.' It was true, they drank in the same pub. Raven had once been invited to the house in Eaton Place where the cabinet of the ghost-government met every two weeks. They claimed to represent ten million Poles in exile but no one else recognized them. They continued stubbornly, unrealistic idealists, supported by money from Canada and the United States.

'These people are my personal friends,' Zaleski said importantly. 'Lamprecht is knowing this.'

Raven's breath left in a sigh. He'd forgotten that Zaleski was immune to sarcasm. His host believed only what pleased him and then implicitly. Nothing shook his faith. The antics of the C.I.A. and K.G.B. might read like fiction but for Zaleski they were obviously real. He saw nothing incongruous in the fact that such people's interest would centre on a bunch of raffish expatriates.

'I'm going to give you some good advice,' said Raven. 'Don't make a fool of yourself.'

'*Fool?*' repeated Zaleski.

Background music filtered into Raven's hearing. A woman's laugh, Chopin, a distant crash from the kitchen. Zaleski was a romantic from a different age.

'Listen,' Raven said gently. 'Let's get this thing in perspective. People living on a border of another country are bound to have their accents affected. Why *should* people know the man? He could have come here from anywhere.'

Zaleski destroyed the suggestion with a monitory finger. 'The girl lives in Waverley Court.'

'I know,' said Raven.

Zaleski poured himself another shot of vodka. The ice around the bottle was beginning to melt.

'So you are still being bloody inspector-detective.'

'Not really,' Raven replied. 'It was on my way. A kind of sentimental journey. I stopped outside your flat for the sake of the bad old days. She was coming out.'

The Pole's shoulders rose and fell. His tone was compassionate. 'She is in love with me.'

This was vintage Zaleski. 'Of course,' said Raven. 'You're too yummy not to be loved. But she's not your type. I can tell. You've caused enough havoc with women in your time. Give this one a break,' he urged.

Zaleski's voice and manner were stiff with drink but he rode the irony as a gull does stormy water.

'Lamprecht is using her. I ask you one favour, Pan John. Is not too much for old comrades.'

Raven spread his hands. It had been a good meal and there were times to be generous.

'What do you want?'

Zaleski uncovered a piece of paper hidden under his hand. He pushed it across the table.

'Two nights ago. Putting address on back of cheque. Ask your friends.'

The tablecloth slipped under the movement of his elbows. He just managed to catch the ashtray before it hit the ground. Raven looked down at the slip of paper. Justice Place.

'I'm promising nothing,' he warned.

Zaleski was on his feet, folding Raven in a bear-hug. 'K.G.B.,' he whispered and belched. He rolled as far as the door with Raven.

CHAPTER TWO

Raven, Tuesday

Lamprecht's address was a short stretch of flagged pavement between a dozen Queen Anne-style houses. There were patches of grass in front and the warm night was heavy with the smell of roses. Hidden behind a churchyard and barred to traffic the place was remote from the noise and strobe-lights of Kings Road. A perambulator had been left in one of the gardens. Curtains and blinds were undrawn, windows open. Number eleven was the last house but one on the left side. Raven stopped and took his time lighting a cigarette. The interior of the first-floor room was illuminated by a pedestal lamp. Shelves filled with books covered one wall. Still more books were piled beneath a table bearing a bronze horse and a telephone.

He leaned against the brick wall smoking and listening to the sound of a harpsichord. Someone was playing Landowska. It was strange the way that curiosity patterned one's life. There was no real reason why he should stand outside a stranger's house, stare through his windows and disturb his privacy. Zaleski had been drunk. Not staggering drunk perhaps but enough to fan the flames of an already wild imagination. Count of the Holy Roman Empire, no less. Beloved of beautiful women and now tracked by the K.G.B.

The record ended, leaving the sound of a man's voice calling for coffee. Raven scratched at his gnat-bites, trying

to remember if there was salve in the medicine chest.
Instinct told him that Lamprecht's house was empty. The
downstairs light had probably been left on intentionally.
At least the thinking was imaginative. Villains on the
prowl were no longer put off by the solitary lamp left
burning in the hallway. It was a civilized room, he thought.
Red carnations in a vase, books, the dull gleam of silver.
An unlikely setting for a K.G.B. agent. No, Zaleski was
really too much.

He put his heel on the cigarette stub. Home now and
forget the whole thing. A woman's head showed at a window as he made his way back, her face incurious. He had
almost reached the almond tree at the end of the wide
passage when a taxi stopped on the street beyond. Lamprecht was first out, Barbara Beattie beside him as he paid
off the driver. It was too late for Raven to retreat. The cab
clattered off. The man and woman turned abruptly forcing
Raven to step to one side. The Pole was shorter than Raven
had thought, with dark eyes set in a wedge-shaped face
and short white hair. A man in his late forties. His clothes
were unmistakably English, black shoes and a blue suit.
There was a space of three or four seconds during which
the three of them looked at one another. There was no
doubt about the recognition in Lamprecht's eyes. Barbara
Beattie's face was a mask of hostility.

Raven managed to produce a smile from somewhere,
damning Zaleski, his own curiosity and bad sense of timing.

'Well, good night,' he said hopefully.

Barbara Beattie's glare seemed designed to demolish
him. Whatever words were meant to go with it were left
unsaid. Lamprecht had broken away, white-faced and
clutching his door key. The girl hurried after him. The

slam of the street door echoed down the quiet stretch of houses. Almost immediately the downstairs light was extinguished.

Raven walked home slowly. The river was a wide strip of silver under an upturned sliver of moon. He let himself into the houseboat, his senses lulled by the familiar. There was no salve in the bathroom. He undressed, rubbed vinegar on his bites and walked out on deck in his pyjamas. He was in no mood to listen to music. The scene he had just witnessed didn't make sense. Unless they thought he was some sort of inquiry agent. Maybe one of them was married – or both – and worried about people knowing that they slept together.

He pulled a few discoloured blossoms off the hydrangeas. The stars were out, yellow points of light in a deep purple sky. The floating restaurant had closed. There was no noise, nothing but the soft gurgle of water. He no longer had a woman to come home to but, then, nor did he have to share his bed. He dropped the dead blossoms over the side. It was difficult at times to convince himself that he didn't miss Cathy. There was no one in sight. He went through the motions of his deep-breathing exercises and crawled into bed, reminding himself to ignore Zaleski's next invitation.

He woke as he'd done for years, rested or tired, one eye searching for the pigskin travelling clock. It was just after seven with the morning sun streaming against the curtains. He collected the newspapers from the box at the end of the gangway, yawned his way back to the kitchen, poured boiling water on a teabag and carried the cup back to bed. A bird honked high overhead, a goose perhaps, the sound distinct against the whine of an early incoming jet.

He punched the pillows, closed his eyes and composed himself to think of flight. According to Jerry Soo the trick about meditation was to concentrate on a single thought. He gave up the struggle after a couple of minutes, finding his mind in Acapulco. The hell with it. Maybe you had to be an oriental like Jerry. The steps from there went logically. Jerry, the Yard, information, Lamprecht. He locked his brain firmly against the idea. He was going to do no such thing, he decided. It was a perfect day to go racing and there was a meeting at Sandown. He could get there early, lunch on a cold beer and sandwich and lean against the paddock rails with the rest of them. He'd either win or lose a tenner and come home relaxed. He leafed through the racing sections of the papers, seeking inspiration. Shortly after he was fast asleep again.

A rapping on his door brought him to life. Mrs. Burrows' announcement was uncompromising.

'The 'phone's ringing!'

He pressed the button switching the ringing from the sitting room to his bedside. It was late. Mrs. Burrows didn't come until ten. He lifted the receiver.

'Yes?'

'Mr. Raven?'

'Speaking.' He recognized the voice. It was Barbara Beattie.

She fired the words at him like missiles. 'Just who the hell do you think you are! Do you realize what you've done, you and Zaleski between you? You've driven a sick man to desperation. Well, let me tell you something. You're playing your shabby games with the wrong person.'

A familiar dirge was coming from the kitchen. A version of 'Annie Laurie' known only to Mrs. Burrows.

'Quiet!' he bawled. A door was slammed loudly. He

18

cleared his throat. 'Start again and be civil or I'll hang up on you. What are you talking about?'

He could hear her breathing, then suddenly Zaleski came on. 'Is a bloody mess, John. I'm sorry. Lamprecht has gone.'

The gnat-bites were itching again. The newspapers fluttered to the floor as Raven rubbed his back against the bedhead.

'Gone where?'

'Vanished. Walked out. No goodbye. Just gone.'

'Get off the line,' ordered Raven. 'Let me talk to the girl.'

'He's a sick man,' she repeated. 'I don't care who you are or were. You have absolutely no right to interfere in other people's lives. If anything happens to Henryk you're responsible. And you can bet your last dollar that I'll do my damnedest to make you pay for it.'

He shook his head at her as if she were there in the room. 'You don't sound drunk but you're not making sense. Are you by any chance asking me for some sort of help, Miss Beattie?'

'I want you to know what you've done,' she said stubbornly. 'You and this ridiculous . . . this goddam *windbag*.'

He focused on the woven strips of cane at the end of the bed. 'Windbag' was a description Zaleski wouldn't take kindly.

'Where are you speaking from?'

'Justice Place. You know the house well enough. You were here last night.'

'I'll be there in half-an-hour,' he promised and put the 'phone down.

He opened the kitchen door. Mrs. Burrows was scouring

19

the aluminium sink, presenting an overalled back and a screw of grey hair.

'Peace,' he said, opening the refrigerator. 'It's your turn tomorrow. You can tell me about your lumbago.'

He drank a carton of fruit juice and went back to the bedroom. He shaved, swilled his mouth with peppermint wash and donned jeans, sneakers and a shirt. If he moved fast he could make Sandown. The package of records was still on the worn leather sofa unopened. There was no post and the flowers were dying. He yelled goodbye from the door and went out on deck. The blue Citroën was covered with paw marks. He screwed himself behind the wheel and drove north for a quarter of a mile. Justice Place was bright with sunshine, the perambulator he'd seen the night before placed in the shade of the almond tree. Its occupant thrust a chewed bear over the side. He stooped to pick it up and heard it hit the ground again before he'd reached Lamprecht's gate. The front door was ajar. He stepped into a sunny hallway strewn with scatter-rugs. Straight ahead was a large window with a chestnut-tree in the garden beyond. The staircase was painted white. Barbara Beattie and Zaleski were waiting in the room he had seen from outside. There was a coffee-pot and cups on the table bearing the bronze horse.

Zaleski had changed to grey slacks and a blue shirt, a scarlet cotton scarf tied round his prominent adam's apple. The girl was wearing the same brown linen dress. She looked as if she hadn't slept, lines showing under her faint makeup. Raven felt the coffee-pot. It was hot. He indicated a clean cup.

'Do you mind?'

She shook her head, her mouth and eyes uncertain. Zaleski was in front of the empty fireplace, belly thrust out. He lifted his shoulders and grinned. It was as near embarrassment as he could manage. Raven took his cup to the window. Sunlight picked out titles on the top bookshelf. *Formulae for the Solution of Geometric Transposition Cyphers. The Decline and Fall of the West.*

'O.K.,' he invited. 'Which one of you's going to do the talking?'

The Canadian girl pitched her half-smoked cigarette at the fireplace. 'You,' she said to Zaleski.

The Pole felt for the monocle on the end of its cord. He slotted it under his right eye.

'I was drunk,' he said simply.

Raven put his cup down. He'd forgotten the sugar. 'That's hardly news. Something happened after I left the restaurant. Is that it?'

The monocle dropped. It was obviously doing nothing for Zaleski's composure. He smiled again in the sudden silence, unhelped by either of his listeners.

'Bloody vodka. I told him he was Communist.'

'In Polish and in English.' Barbara Beattie flicked her hair back, her green eyes accusing. 'K.G.B. agent. But your good friend the inspector-detective was on to him.'

'Is that true?' demanded Raven.

Zaleski's upturned palms sought indulgence. Summer sounds drifted in through the open window. Barbara's eyes followed Raven as he returned his cup to the table.

'Why should that have bothered your friend?' he asked quietly. 'We all know Casimir.'

'Why did you come here last night?' she challenged.

He made no answer. If there was a valid one he couldn't think of it.

Her eyes were perfectly steady. 'Haven't you ever heard of someone cracking under stress? Don't you know what it means to love someone who's suffering and not be allowed to help? Henryk's been sick for months – sick in his head. I've had to live with a man who's becoming a stranger, scared of what's happening to his brain. And you stage a scene like last night's. He was literally shaking when we left the restaurant. All he wanted was to get home fast. How do you suppose he felt when we saw you standing there?'

Raven nodded slowly. He was wrong and Zaleski was no excuse for it.

'I'm sorry. If there's anything I can do, tell me. When did he leave – how?'

She lit a cigarette with trembling fingers, face averted, close to tears.

'I was asleep. I felt him get out of bed but I paid no attention. He's been doing this for the last couple of weeks, coming down here and reading then going back to bed. This time it was different. His passport's gone and he's taken his chequebooks. I just got through calling his business before you arrived. He 'phoned them at ten, saying that he'd be away for a week.'

Raven sat down in the sort of chair he liked with a tilted back and arm-rests. He'd taken one into the Yard to a corridor full of cocked eyebrows. It had lasted almost five years till a sour-brained co-ordinator had ordered him to get it out of the building.

'What kind of work does he do?'

'He runs a translation bureau in the City. Polish, Russian, French and German. They specialize in technical documents.'

She opened the rosewood desk behind her and showed the two men an empty drawer.

'That's where he kept his passport.'

'What sort of passport does he have?'

She frowned as though he had said something stupid. 'British, of course. He's been living here since 1956. He was naturalized twelve years ago.'

Raven pointed a finger at Zaleski. The most the Pole had achieved was a limited travel-document.

'You've really excelled yourself, haven't you? K.G.B. You dolt!'

'Watch it, mate,' retorted Zaleski. 'Why being bloody insulting?'

Barbara yanked another drawer open and froze. She turned slowly, holding some snapshots in her hand.

'I don't believe it. I don't understand. Whenever we went away he always took those with him. It's crazy.'

She gave the prints to Raven. They portrayed a woman and baby, and a younger Lamprecht, haunted and unsmiling. Age didn't seem to mellow him. Barbara put the pictures back in the drawer.

'That's his wife and daughter. He married his childhood sweetheart after spending thirteen years in Russian prison camps. They went to Hungary and Henryk got involved in the uprising. The Communists killed his wife and the baby and he came here.'

She spoke with emotion. It was years ago but Raven remembered the influx of refugees, the old and the young, destitute, bewildered, yet somehow hopeful. There'd been a lot of moral indignation, newsreel shots of Soviet tanks in the streets of Budapest, but not a single Western power had moved a division. Barbara closed the desk and leaned back against it, facing them. She was very close to tears.

'Pull yourself together,' urged Raven. 'If he's called his office, he must know what's he's doing. He *could* have gone away for a couple of weeks. Maybe it's as simple as that.'

She shook her head obstinately. 'He's *sick*! You don't seem to be able to get that into your head. He's in no condition to be by himself.'

Zaleski inflated his chest, his voice for once uncertain. 'Now listen, why not . . .?'

'For crissakes keep quiet,' Raven said impatiently. 'Look, Barbara, we're going to help you find him. O.K.?'

She brushed the corners of her eyes with the back of her hand. 'I don't want the police chasing him if that's what you mean. He's been through too much for that.'

'No police,' promised Raven. 'The police aren't obliged to look for people over 17. Just you, Casimir and me. The first thing we have to know is what's wrong with him. What's the name of his doctor?'

She swept one side of her hair back, offering a glimpse of the fineboned line from temple to chin.

'Do you think I'd be standing here if I knew? He'd never tell me. Even the pills he took were kept secret, hidden away in a drawer in his dressing room. He's taken those too. The drawer's unlocked.'

Raven considered the toes of his stained sneakers, conscious of her unvoiced appeal. The hostility had gone and he was being asked for help.

'How about your job? Can you take time off?'

She moved her shoulders indifferently. 'I already have. I don't care about the job. I just want to find Henryk before something happens.'

The child under the almond tree was bawling its head off. Zaleski shut the window, bringing quiet to the book-lined room. Raven was thinking of white rails and green turf, the smell of horseflesh. He put the picture out of his

mind regretfully. The Canadian girl fished in her handbag and used a small mirror to repair her smudged makeup. She reminded him of Cathy in a way. She had the same
slow reluctant smile. But this woman was a survivor. And
rightly or wrongly he'd just given her his word. He
jumped as the 'phone shrilled suddenly. Barbara looked
across at him, her fingers at her throat.

'Answer it,' he instructed. With any luck it would be
Lamprecht and he'd still be able to make Sandown.

She picked up the 'phone. 'Hello?'

She covered the mouthpiece with her palm. 'It's
Henryk's bank. They want to talk to him.'

'Say you're a friend,' he said quickly. 'He's just gone
out. Ask if you can take a message.'

She nodded and spoke with newfound assurance. After
a couple of minutes she hung up, her eyes seeking Raven's.

'An estate agent's been trying to get hold of him. He
gave the bank as reference. They want to know when it
would be convenient for a man to check the guttering.'

'*Here?*' He knew the answer before she opened her
mouth.

She moved her head from side to side. 'Swan Lodge,
River Way, Hampton Court.'

He jumped up, brushing off the lint from the worn
velvet cushion. 'O.K. Let's go.'

CHAPTER THREE

Lamprecht, Wednesday

It was almost six o'clock with the rising sun lightening the
sky to the east. A grey cat jumped, landing with its tail

lashing, its unwinking gaze on the sparrows in the almond tree. There was no other movement in the row of sleeping houses. Lamprecht tiptoed from the window. Barbara was huddled on the bed, one freckled shoulder free of the green-striped sheets, red hair covering her face. Her breathing was deep and regular.

He dressed hurriedly, donning dark-grey flannel trousers and rubber-soled shoes. He unlocked a drawer in the maple tallboy. The two small phials of blue pills were almost full, ample for his needs at four a day. He put the bottle in his pocket, crept down the stairs and let himself out of the house very quietly. He glanced right and left, dragging the untainted air deep into his lungs. The cat had disappeared. There was no one to watch as he walked quickly towards the corner, his feet making no sound on the flagged pavement.

It was a long time since he had been hunted. The old fears revived the exhilaration of living on the edge of danger. He responded, sweaty-palmed and dry-mouthed, aware of doorways, trees, the cars parked on both sides of the road, even the milk-float gliding towards him, electrically propelled. He changed direction on impulse and headed towards the river. The shock of the previous night persisted. The drunken Pole with his wild accusations, the gaunt sinister policeman waiting outside the house. A detective-inspector, Zaleski had said. It was the sort of scene he had been dreading for the past ten days, an involvement with authority, explanations – the chance happening that could so easily defeat his purpose. There were still twenty-four hours to go and he was on his own now, wherever he went, whatever he did. There was no question of asking for help, least of all from the girl he had left in his bed. Barbara's love was too protective, too much concerned with living, to accept the truth. He could only act and hope for understanding.

There was practically no traffic along the Embankment, nothing but the first run of lorries lumbering north, no taxis. He crossed on the green light with a lone cyclist locked in some dream of the Tour de France. The houseboats below to the right clustered against the north bank while off in the other direction the three bridges spanned the majestic Thames. Beyond them were the towering highrise buildings of Victoria and, in the shadow of New Scotland Yard, the edifice where his double life was led. Sixteen hours a week, four tours of duty.

Battersea Park was still closed. The bus emerging from the garage was going the wrong way. He walked west towards the helicopter landing-pad. He could have collected his car but the storage floors wouldn't be open. The car had been there for the last two months, since the morning Holland had delivered his verdict. It had been a muggy day in April with the consulting-room uncomfortably hot. Rain tapped at the windows as the specialist droned on dispassionately.

I have to agree with the previous opinions. The tumour is set in the central area of the dominant hemisphere and is inoperable. I suspect that it is larger than we think, infiltrating between the nerve fibres. This would account for the failure of memory and what you describe as a 'feeling of unreality'. In other words a change of personality. I'm afraid that there just isn't any satisfactory form of treatment. I see that Professor Cullen has recommended radium radiation. Quite frankly I'm against it. Degeneration of tissue and haemorrhage are inevitable. I'd sooner have you running on all cylinders, so to speak, albeit slowly.

The 'phone had rung and Holland had answered it, returning to Lamprecht's question with spatulate fingertips pressed together.

How long? Well, there are no criteria that are completely diagnostic. But there are definite time limits. The average length of life is twelve months from the first onset.

He had closed the file, looking away as Lamprecht worked it out. The first attack had come in November, a blinding flash of pain that had left him terrified. He had seven months to live. It was strange to go on as if nothing had happened. There was no one to share his thoughts with. He had no friends, mistrusting the British at heart and despising the expatriate Poles. Decadent romantics like Zaleski, whining that the world owed them fame and honour with no real claim to either. His religion had gone in Russia so there wasn't even the comfort of the confessional. And Barbie's heart was too exposed to stab. He'd lived under sentence of death like a man waiting for the gallows, resentful and somehow shamed, until chance had given him the perfect answer.

A corner shop was open, selling cigarettes, newspapers and soft drinks. He bought a Coke and used it to wash down a couple of the bright blue pills. Another twenty minutes and the pain behind his left eye would vanish. He suspected a morphine derivative but was grateful to a compassionate general practitioner. It was almost eight by the time he reached Putney High Street. The houses and blocks of flats on the hill were emptying, the occupants joining the first massive assault on public transport. He stood in the station entrance, jostled by the surging crowd, scanning the passing faces for a sign of danger. Satisfied that no one was following him, he shouldered his way out to a cab parked in the middle of the road.

'Hampton Court Bridge. The south side.'

The driver pulled the flag down and folded his news-paper. Lamprecht leaned back, shutting his eyes. He'd slept little, feigning unconsciousness whenever Barbara moved. He could rest for a while in the house. He was safe there. Nobody knew of its existence. Barbie was bound to contact the office but they were used to his absences. In any case the bureau ran itself. He'd call Sara Moffatt and tell her that he'd be away for a week. There was plenty of work and the monthly pay-cheques were signed. The important area was the Centre. Burke was security officer for the week so there could be no suggestion of nervousness, nothing that could give them a clue to what was coming.

He walked behind the vanishing cab till it was out of sight and ran down a flight of stone steps leading to the towpath. He passed a couple of fishermen, an elderly man drinking tea from a thermos flask, a young boy intent on his drifting float. A dog's bark and the sound of children calling came from the meadows on the far side of the water. On past boathouses that were painted white, to willows that hid the end of the towpath. A wooden notice board hung on the iron fence:

NO FISHING   NO BATHING
TRESPASSERS WILL BE PROSECUTED
By order of the Thames Conservancy Board

He climbed the fence, using the board as a hand- and foot-hold, and dropped down into lush grass. The reservoir lay on his left, the unruffled surface of the water reflecting the blue of the sky. He headed towards the distant trees keeping as close to the bank as he could. Mute swans hissed with extended necks protecting their cygnets. He was near enough to the house now to be safe if stopped. He could say he was looking for a dog that had slipped through the railings. His fears were unfounded. The only shouts were those of the children behind. There was nothing to help him scale the second barrier. The notice board was broken. He worked his way to the end, flanking the spiked frieze sticking out into the water. The earth between the alders and willows was spongy and smelled faintly of gas. Five minutes took him through the spinney to the hole he had made in the thick box-hedge. He went through it backwards, hands protecting his face from the small stiff leaves.

The house was Thames-side Edwardian, a one-storey building constructed of soft red brick. The paint on the iron veranda was peeling and moles had thrown up mounds of chocolate-coloured earth on the lawn that sloped down to the rushes. A stand of beech trees blocked the view from the neighbouring house but he ducked low, keeping to the unkempt flowerbeds. He had rented the house through an agency:

TO LET FOR A SHORT PERIOD
OWNER GOING ABROAD
A SECLUDED PROPERTY COMPRISING THREE
BEDROOMS AND TWO RECEPTION ROOMS
TOGETHER WITH THE USUAL OFFICES

He'd viewed it at once, ignoring the shabby furniture and damp stains as well as the agent's hurried patter. The place was ideal. It was reached at the front from a narrow lane with the backwater and reservoir offering lines of escape. An opportunity to research a book, he'd said, agreeing the exorbitant rent. He'd given a cheque against damages and tenancy and collected the keys the following week. Since then he'd been to the house on five occasions, three times at night, carrying the brown canvas bag with his tools and materials.

Potma had been no place for a Polish prisoner-of-war to be stupid if he wanted to live. Lamprecht had learned his trade well, assembling electronic equipment and stealing the odd component till at the end he had a simple but effective radio hidden in the compound latrines. It was the only place the Russians didn't search thoroughly. Lamprecht had crouched there, early on a May morning in 1945, listening to the excited gabble of the announcer. Berlin had just fallen to the invincible forces of the U.S.S.R. The news brought hope to the Poles. They had fought against the Germans and were allies of the West. Ten years later, Lamprecht was still using the same lavatory-seat and radio.

He stood for a while, looking at the blinds beyond the dirty window panes. Bees droned in the honeysuckle by his head. A tall wooden-slatted fence separated the sun-soaked yard from the tarmac in front of the house. The gate was locked and bolted. He used his keys to let himself into the kitchen. Nothing had been moved since his last visit. The dead flies were still on the sills, the spider in the sink. The mirror above the refrigerator reminded him that he hadn't shaved. There was a razor and toothbrush in the bathroom. He had kept to the back of the house since making the first inspection, using only the chintz-furnished bedroom and musty drawing room. He opened the refrigerator. The light came on inside. Coffee and sugar were hidden with the milk. He waited till the pipes cleared of rust before running water into a pan. He made coffee as he had done as a boy, boiling the crushed beans and throwing in a chip of wood to settle the grounds. He carried the cup into the drawing room and sat by the cob-webbed windows. The agents had been surprised at his hasty tenancy, offering to have the house cleaned but accepting his invention of a faithful housekeeper. There were family portraits on a table, a man and woman in formal wedding-attire, the same couple gazing down at a child in a cradle, a fat girl on a pony. Against the rain-blotched wall was a grand piano with yellowed keys. The carpet was stained. He took off his tie and lit a cigarette. The airless room smelled of mice and disuse. He hadn't opened a window in all his visits, even waiting for the noise of a passing car before flushing the lavatory cistern. He reasoned that someone might be walking along the lane outside and hear. He wanted the house to appear as it had for the last fifteen months, unoccupied.

He smoked, watching the blackbird on the lawn, and remembering that it would be twenty years exactly next week. He could still run the film of events in his mind – Budapest. He'd made his way home from the meeting, the sound of tank-guns in his ears, crossing empty railway tracks, running close to factory walls that were daubed with anti-Russian slogans. The street where he lived with his wife and infant daughter had been deserted, the pavements strewn with huddled bodies and empty shell-cases. A burnt-out tram lay on its side at the intersection. The sun that had shone that morning was still in his brain even now, an angry disc turned copper by the pall above the beleaguered city. Nothing moved in the yellow apart-ment building as he entered. The lights were out. Power had failed the previous night, trapping the lift between floors. Hands reached from behind, pulling him into a doorway as he started up the concrete staircase. The same hands covered his mouth, holding him tight as footsteps ran across the hallway. A voice called and was answered in Russian. Seconds later a car pulled away.

A man's face showed in the half-light of drawn curtains. He spoke in Hungarian, his eyes compassionate.

'They are dead, my poor friend. Everyone living on the floor is dead. Eighteen of them. The bastards came at five this morning with machine guns. They were looking for you.'

The blackbird scurried away. Lamprecht searched his pockets for another cigarette. He no longer wept, though sorrow had etched his memory. Time had given him a source of parallel justice and he'd sought information from the archives. He'd seen the smuggled pictures of the bloodstained apartments, the bullet-riddled bodies that lay so grotesquely. Yet his mind had always refused death for his daughter. She was alive and well somewhere, his own flesh and blood who would never know him. And now a miracle had been wrought, a miracle giving him the chance to avenge her mother's murder.

He brewed more coffee and took it to the bedroom. The lowered blind diffused the strong sunshine, bathing the room in a pale amber light. There were no sheets on the bed, folded blankets stacked on top of a brassbound chest. The only attempt at decoration was a blackframed oil of a Labrador hanging on faded regency-striped wallpaper. He put the cup and pan on the dressing table. The canvas bag was under the bed. He pulled it between his legs and unzipped the top. The machine inside was the size of a large portable typewriter with two keyboards. One bore the letters of the Cyrillic alphabet, the other the numerals one to nine. There were two buttons marked START-

STOP and DECODE. He lifted the machine onto the bed beside him and unscrewed the heavy plastic base. The electrical circuits were traced silver and brown on the face of the transistorized chassis. He chose a screwdriver with its head set at right angles to the shank and undid the chassis. A slim aluminium box was fastened to the base of the keyboards. The box was the size of two cigarette packages placed end to end and to all intents and purposes an integral part of the machine. The cap detonator next to it was concealed in a transistor casing.

He tested the contacts carefully, renewing one lead and soldering it into place. Then he reassembled the machine, plugged the cable into a wall-socket and thumbed the start button. A small red light shone on one side of the keyboards. He switched off the power and returned the device to the bag. It was impressive enough to fool anyone except an absolute expert and the odds were against him meeting one. All he needed was access to the embassy. He'd done his homework carefully, checking figures against known records. Five hundred grams of plastic explosive would produce a force powerful enough to completely destroy anything in its immediate vicinity. He'd collected the plastic in Paris ten days before, from a locker in the Gare St. Lazare. He'd left the price in French francs and returned the locker key to the blind Malinowski. Neither of them had spoken. After sharing a cell for four years assurance was unnecessary. Now, activated by the secret switch he'd installed, the explosive was ready to do its job.

He finished the last of the coffee and shaved in the bathroom. The message hadn't specified Butov's route, only the date of his arrival in London. The 18 Directorate missive had originated in Rome and enjoined secrecy, using the code name Butov had worn for the past twelve years. He'd almost certainly fly in by Aeroflot, picking up a Russian plane in either Zürich or Geneva. Lamprecht put his shaving things back in their case and thoroughly cleaned the handbasin. Tonight would be his last tour of duty at the Centre. He dared not risk another even if he hadn't made full contact with the Russians by tomorrow. Four until eight, the 'tea-dancing shift' as Burke called it. After almost nineteen years in the country Lamprecht was still unable to understand the British. Burke was an enigma. Personnel at the Centre were forbidden to meet socially, discouraged from discussing their private lives and known to each other only by their cover-names. Something Burke had once said suggested the schoolmaster. And the manner was there, the patronage, the hint of superior knowledge, and heavy attempts at humour.

Back in the drawing room he sat in the sagging arm-chair with the writing pad open across his knees. It was better to compose the letter now while his thoughts were comparatively clear. He wrote slowly, destroying his first drafts and reading his final effort with a complete sense of hopelessness. He was asking for absolution without having made a full confession. So much of what he should have said remained locked up inside him.

He was addressing the envelope when the 'phone bell shattered the peace of the house and brought him bolt up-right in his chair. His first impulse was to stifle the sound with a cushion. Nobody knew he was there. The place was supposed to be empty and a passer-by might be curious. He rose and backed off, dry-mouthed as the 'phone con-tinued to ring, the table it was on acting as a sounding board. Then suddenly all was silent. He let his breath go, the shrill summons still ringing in his ears. There were two 'phones. The other was in the bedroom. He hadn't used either on any of his visits. He stared down uncertainly at the envelope he was holding, his mind hurtling back over the precautions he had taken. It was impossible that anyone could know he was here. No one knew of his tenancy apart from the estate agents and he was sure that he hadn't been followed. The call had to be misrouted.

He reached the end of the corridor just in time to hear the 'phone ringing again, this time from the bedroom, as if the unknown caller was following his movements. The pain behind his left eye had started up again, blurring his vision and invading his mastoids. He sat down heavily on the side of the bed, heart banging in his ribcage. The ringing stopped as suddenly as it began and the pain gradually subsided. He tiptoed to a front room and peeped through a chink in the blind. The leafy lane was completely deserted except for a small black van parked about thirty yards away. He could just read the lettering on the side. MAYFIELD TELEVISION. The man at the wheel lowered his newspaper and glanced in Lamprecht's direction. Lamprecht stepped back hurriedly, adrenalin pumping alarm to his brain. *It was the man from the restaurant, Zaleski's friend.* He looked again and the grey-blond hair became a cloth cap. A stranger was innocently eating a sandwich. Lamprecht wiped the back of his hand across his mouth. The place was getting on top of him. Movement was better. He was going to have to sleep here but by then it would be dark. He retrieved the canvas bag from the bedroom and let himself out through the kitchen. The blackbird on the lawn waited in the dappled shade of a chestnut tree, unafraid of Lamprecht's invasion of its territory.

He opened the rickety door to the boathouse. It was built on stilts and overgrown by alder shoots. A holed punt lay submerged below the surface of the black water. He made his way to the end of the platform and hid the bag under a pile of rotting sails. It was almost eleven. He'd use the first 'phone he found to call the bureau.

The concrete walls of the reservoir glittered in the sunshine and the wide stretch of water was without a ripple. There was no one in sight as he clambered round the end of the railings and leaped for the towpath. He landed awkwardly, unbalanced. These damned dizzy spells were becoming more frequent, two or three a day sometimes. They'd warned him that this would be possible, even a form of convulsion, that he'd almost certainly survive the first cerebral insult. *Cerebral insult* – the words were from some strange book of gobbledygook. He had destroyed the card they had given him to carry along with the rest of the *macabre* dossier. The X-ray pictures, the diagnoses typed in technical language, Dr. Belling's delicately-worded explanation of them.

He opened his eyes gradually, as he'd done as a drunken youth, kneeling on his bed and waiting for the room to stop spinning. A fish plopped near the bank, missing its strike at a bug. A hidden bird was singing in the willows. He'd never see another summer or spring. The thought left him deeply melancholy. He straightened his head and body, the dizziness gone. He hadn't eaten since the night before and needed food in his stomach. He made his way along the bank to the bridge and climbed the stone steps. A bus full of tourists had stopped at the top. He pushed on past clicking cameras to the 'phone box outside the Underground station. He dialled a number and fed a coin into the slot. A girl's voice answered. 'Universal Translations, Sara Moffatt speaking. Good morning.'

'Lamprecht,' he said. He had perfected his English to

the point where he thought in the language unconsciously. 'Look, I have to be away on business. There's nothing particular you want me for, is there?'

He could hear the battery of electric typewriters in the background. 'I don't think so, no,' she replied. 'How long are you going for, Mr. Lamprecht?'

'I'm not quite sure, a few days probably. Have there been any 'phone calls for me?'

'Just a minute, I'll ask.' She spoke to someone else in the room. 'Just Miss Beattie. She 'phoned about half an hour ago. She said she'd call back. Is there any message'

'No message,' he said quickly. 'I'll be in touch at the end of the week.'

He crossed the street to the pub opposite. It was Guinness Georgian with wooden benches outside. A woman in tight satin with a dyed blonde beehive looked up from her crossword puzzle. There was nobody else in the bar.

'Yes, please.'

A card offered the menu. Cold and hot snacks served from twelve to two. It was just about noon. He selected a plate of cold cuts and salad from the glass case and ordered a lager. Condemned men didn't always have what they wanted. Beer and wine were allowed but Dr. Belling had forbidden spirits. He forced himself to eat the tasteless meat and limp lettuce. Suddenly the door to the street swung open. The barmaid folded her newspaper hurriedly. The customer was a man in his late fifties with protruding eyes in a red pugnacious face. He was wearing a rakish hat, a conservatively-cut suit with a rosebud in his lapel, and smelled strongly of liquor. He limped in on one brogue shoe and one carpet slipper. His smile flashed on and off like a ventriloquist's doll's.

'A large Scotch, Millie. Make it two.'

He tipped one glass into the other and leaned against the bar favouring the leg with the carpet slipper. The terrifying smile came and went again, aimed at Lamprecht.

'Haven't seen you in here before, have I? But then I've been laid up with the gout, you know.'

The woman had moved away behind him and was shaking her head significantly. Lamprecht took his time lighting a cigarette. The man limped over and sat down at Lamprecht's table. His veined face looked as if it had been starched.

'My name's Bowles. How do you do, sir!'

Lamprecht nodded uneasily. 'Good morning.'

Bowles glanced at him sharply. 'Foreigner, are you? Where do you come from?'

A man in his shirtsleeves had joined the barmaid. They were both looking across the room.

An impression of evil had invaded the bar and Lamprecht was aware of the tension.

'I'm Polish originally,' he explained. 'A British subject now.'

Bowles drained his glass, refilled it and limped back to the table. 'And what did you do to become a British citizen?'

'I was naturalized,' said Lamprecht.

'Then you must wear a rose, a rose for England.' Bowles had the bud from his lapel, offering it to Lamprecht with a nicotine-stained smile.

Lamprecht accepted it doubtfully. The man was obviously drunk. 'What do you do for a living?' said Bowles, cigarette jumping in the corner of his mouth as he spoke.

Something in Lamprecht's brain told him to be careful but he couldn't bring himself to get up and go.

'I think that's my business,' he said quietly.

Bowles removed his hat and dropped ash into it without appearing to know what he'd done.

'Let me explain something,' he said, hiccuping. 'I control the vote in this area as these people will tell you.'

The landlord was pantomiming with his finger against the side of his head.

'Please go away,' said Lamprecht. 'I'd like to finish my beer in peace.'

The landlord's voice was cajoling. 'Now then, Major. The gentleman doesn't want to be bothered.'

Bowles was up quickly in spite of his disability. He jammed his hat back on his head, the ash inside streaking his greasy face.

'I've had to kill men with my bare hands,' he snarled. 'While you fuckers were skulking in bomb shelters. British citizen be buggered! I'll bet he's a Bolshy.'

The landlord ducked under the flap in the bar. 'That's enough. I don't like your language or your custom. Out!'

'Don't you put a finger on me,' warned Bowles. 'A word to the Regional Crime Squad and I can have you closed tomorrow.'

'Out!' repeated the landlord, opening the door to the street.

Bowles swung in the doorway, pointing at Lamprecht. 'We know your sort – a bad breed. And I don't forget a face. You're a marked man from now on.'

The landlord put his foot against the door as if expecting Bowles to barge back in.

'I'm sorry about that,' he said to Lamprecht. 'The Major's got a bee in his pocket, you know, reds under the beds and all that. Sorry. Let me get you another drink.'

Lamprecht's glass had been overturned somehow. The rosebud lay in a small pool of beer. He shook his head, wanting only to be gone. It had been a long time since a stranger attacked him and now it had happened twice in two days. First Zaleski, now this drunken oaf. It was as if he carried with him some sign that infuriated them. Like a sane man locked away in a lunatic asylum he had to be on guard every second.

He left by the far door. He'd acted too hastily running away from the house as he had done. He could as easily have told Barbie some story about being away on business. The threat wouldn't come from her but from that policeman. It was the way they worked, using the chance word overheard to vent their mistrust. It didn't matter that in this case the accusation would be hopelessly wrong. Having to explain who he was and what he did would ruin his chances. All he needed was a day and a night free of trouble, the last tour of duty at the Code and Cypher Centre. He dared not risk a break in his routine there. It was essential that he turn up for work as usual.

CHAPTER FOUR

Raven, Wednesday

They drove in the Citroën, Zaleski in front with Raven and the girl behind. Raven passed the street map back over his shoulder.

'Find out which bridge we need.'

She kicked off her shoes, drawing up her legs and tucking her dress over them like a small girl. She flicked through the pages to the maps.

'Hampton Court.' Her voice and manner were strained.

41

He glanced up at the rearview mirror. 'Well, don't look at me like that,' he complained. 'I'm here and I've apologized. What more do you want?'

There was sweat in the hollow of her throat and her forehead was wet. She shook a sweep of dark red hair behind her left ear and held it there.

'I don't know how a thing like this can happen. All his life he's had to fight and now this. It's incredible.'

'No courage,' Zaleski said importantly. He was sitting bolt upright with his arms folded across his chest. 'You see, in *my* life . . .'

'For crissakes belt up,' retorted Raven. 'We all know about your life.'

Zaleski closed his small deepset eyes, his face a mask of resignation. They approached the bridge from the Twickenham side. Oars flashed on the river below, the crew naked to the waist and rowing against the current. Zaleski's eyes were open again, giving the oarsmen the benefit of his judgement.

Barbara Beattie leaned forward suddenly, her hands on the back of Raven's seat. 'Over there – by the pub!'

Raven swung the wheel hard. There was an empty car park behind the mock-tudor pub. A sign beyond indicated a hidden turning. He drove into the leafy tunnel. Bright sunshine pierced the dense foliage in places, dappling the narrow lane. It was strangely peaceful, a wooded triangle hidden in the bend of the Thames. Houses showed through the trees on both sides. He braked, seeing the shingles on the gate protecting the quarter-circle of the drive. Swan Lodge was a sprawling one-storey building on the river fronted by overgrown rhododendron bushes. Time and weather had plastered debris across the bottom of the entrance. Blinds sagged at half-mast in grimy windows and the place looked deserted. The lane curved, ending abruptly in a nursery garden. Half-an-acre of glass glittered in the sunlight. Raven reversed and killed the motor. A board in the long grass offered shrubs and plants for sale. Spray from sprinklers cooled the air, drifting down on splashes of colour in dark moist dirt. The sound of a recorder and the babble of children came from the open windows of the play school opposite. Beyond that was the river.

Raven twisted round in his seat. Barbara was pushing long slender feet into the straps of her shoes, the movement moulding the shape of the breasts beneath the brown linen.

'O.K.,' he said quietly. 'What exactly do you want to do?'

She looked at him uncertainly, frown lines creasing her fine freckled skin.

'I just want to find him.'

He pushed his hand out on impulse. She took it and clung to it tightly for a couple of seconds, her green eyes pleading.

'Help me!'

He nodded assurance, responding to the confession of vulnerability. 'Let's get it out in the open,' he suggested gently. 'What is it you're really afraid of – that he's going to commit suicide?'

She narrowed her gaze as if he had struck her but her eyes stayed steady. 'I just want to find him,' she repeated doggedly.

'That's what we're here for,' said Raven. 'The thing is, are you going to trust me?'

She gave him the slow rueful smile that reminded him of Cathy. 'I guess I have to, don't I?'

He shifted his weight, hanging still further over the back of the seat.

'You don't have to do anything. If you want me to split then I'll split. Casimir can stay with you.'

Zaleski belched softly and rapped his belly with the heel of his hand. She made a small quick gesture that drew them together.

'Please!'

'That's better,' said Raven. 'Then here's what you do. You saw the house. I want you to go back there and knock on the door. When he opens it, throw your arms round him and tell him you love him. Tell him it's all a mistake, that people only want to leave him alone.'

She hesitated for the time it took to take a small mirror from the brown suede bag beside her. She used her lipstick with sure deft strokes, rolled her mouth and smiled.

'O.K., you're on. If I'm not back in ten minutes just leave us. Both of you. That's all I ask.'

She walked away with quick strides that sent her shoulder-length hair swinging. Zaleski's eyes followed her fondly.

'Is extrimly attractive girl. If I am paying more attention to her then no bloody Lamprecht. I am responsible.'

Raven swung sideways in disbelief. 'For God's sake give it a rest. She wouldn't look at you on a desert island.'

Zaleski's secret smile flouted the suggestion. 'You are like bloody Bourbons, learn nothing and forget nothing. You'll see, mate. When all this is over, you'll see.'

Raven opened his door, staring at the Pole with open incredulity. A Bonnie Prince Charlie was hidden deep in the other man's psyche.

'Bullshit,' Raven said shortly and strolled into the dappled shade of the beech trees. Dandelions grew in the grass verges. The children's voices pursued him, a reminder that he hadn't seen his nephew and niece in months. The thought left him with a vague feeling of dissatisfaction. If only people would leave him alone. His sister, Zaleski, this girl. Right now he should be at Sandown, working out form with a cold beer and a smoked salmon sandwich inside him. In a little more than a year he'd be forty with his life half-lived. And what had he got to show for it? Take away the trust money, money he'd never earned, and what was left? What had he ever achieved? He trod squarely in a pile of dogshit and wiped his sneakers on the verge. A sense of humour, that's what was left, he decided. He looked up, hearing the noise of someone coming. Barbara hurried around the bend, her face distressed as she hurried to meet him. He took her arm, walked her to the car and climbed in beside her.

'O.K., what happened?'

She dabbed a tissue on the bloody scratches on her forearm. 'I tried the front door and banged on the windows. The side gate is locked. There's nobody in the house. No one.'

'There will be,' he promised. 'What we have to do now is get this car off the road out of sight.'

An Airedale puppy was lying asleep in front of the house next to Swan Lodge. The front door was wide open, offering a view of a white-panelled hall, french windows and the lawn beyond. Raven pulled the car into the shade of the beech trees that fringed the red-brick building.

'Wait over there. I'll be back in a couple of minutes.'

He left the Citroën in the yard behind the pub, vaulted the rails and returned to the lane. Zaleski and the girl were standing in the drive.

He beckoned them to join him and leaned his weight

tentatively against the front door. The paint was blistered and cracked, the metal parts of the locks dull and unscratched. He shook his head.

'It's been a long time since anyone came in this way. He has to be using the back door.'

Zaleski slotted in his monocle and bent, inspecting the two locks narrowly.

'A strong piece of plastic,' he said knowingly, indicating the Yale. 'Is easy.'

Raven looked at him witheringly. 'Where'd they teach you that, in Brixton Prison?' Zaleski was beginning to get on his nerves again. 'Keep an eye on him,' he said to the girl. 'I'll see if I can get us into the place.'

He pushed through the tangle of rhododendron bushes, got over the tall slatted fence and climbed into a small yard paved with the same soft red brick that had built the house. A giant hollyhock drooped over a grey plastic dustbin. The honeysuckle on the wall was alive with bees. He peered through the dirty kitchen windows. A yellowed newspaper on the draining board beside the sink was eight months old. The clock on the wall had stopped and there was no food to be seen, no sign that the house was occupied except that the key had been removed from the mortise lock. He opened a crack in the door at the rear of the yard. A hundred yards of ragged lawn stretched to a derelict boathouse at the edge of the river. The garden had the still enchanted appearance that comes when it is deserted. A blackbird eyed Raven unafraid from the hedge.

He took another look at the window. It was the sort that opened outwards on a ratchet. He prised a brick from the paving and clouted the window frame close to the catch. The screws gave in the rotten wood. He climbed into the aluminium sink and refastened the window as best he could. He whirled as the refrigerator suddenly came into life. There was nothing inside it except coffee, sugar and milk.

A corridor ran the length of the house divided by a central hall. A pile of letters and handouts lay on the mat just inside the front door. He moved them around with the toe of his sneaker. The letters looked for the most part like bills. Cards advertised car hire firms, twenty-four-hour plumbers and contract office cleaners. There was nothing addressed to Lamprecht. He undid the chain and slipped back the catch of the Yale lock. The other two came in quickly, Zaleski drawing in his belly and ducking his head as Barbara preceded him. Raven shut the door again and put the chain on. It was dim after the brightness outside, the air stale and lifeless. The silence was almost tangible. It was Zaleski who broke it, grunting and wagging his head disparagingly as he looked around.

'What did you expect?' asked Raven. 'The Savoy?'

Zaleski made a face behind the girl's back, muttering, 'Is getting bloody Poles bad name.'

Raven showed him two fingers. He led the way along the corridor, opening one door after another. There were two chintz-curtained bedrooms, the smaller one obviously a child's. The blankets were piled on top of one another and there were no sheets. The bath and lavatory were streaked with rust. Barbara pointed at the leather razor case and tooth-brush on the ledge beneath the mirror.

'Lamprecht?' queried Raven.

She nodded, her teeth nipping her lower lip. It was the first real piece of evidence that linked the missing Pole to the house. There were only two more rooms, both on the other side of the corridor. A dining room with stiff uncomfortable chairs and plush curtains ravaged by moths hanging in the french windows. The last room was the largest, musty and smelling of mice. Their droppings littered the warped top of a grand piano. The candles in the glass containers had been chewed to the wick. Wind had driven rain through the cracks in the windows and damp mapped the walls. Zaleski blew hard at a picture of a couple looking into a bassinet.

'Gemütlich!'

Raven and the girl moved in the same instant, both reaching for the envelope on the table. He took his hand away, seeing her name on it. She broke the seal slowly, staring at him as if unwilling to remove whatever was inside.

'What are you waiting for?' he asked. 'Go ahead and read it.'

The envelope fluttered to the floor. She carried its contents to the window, holding the single sheet of paper to the light. She must have read it five or six times, her lips moving as if the words were sour in her mouth. She brushed her hair back quickly with the now familiar gesture, her voice unexpectedly loud.

'I don't understand. I don't understand what he's saying.'

He took the letter from her hand. It was short to the point of curtness, the language almost brutal in its formality apart from the opening phrase.

Barbara, my dear,

This is to say goodbye. Your life has been one long search for love. The tragedy is that I should be the one to fail you. I have never been able to match your generosity of spirit, your selflessness. The end is near,

48

Barbara, and there are secrets that I cannot share. I can only say that I do what I must and beg your forgiveness.

Henryk.

Zaleski was peering over his shoulder. 'I am at your side always,' he said to the girl.

'That's no big deal,' she answered scathingly. 'Is somebody going to tell me what he means?' she demanded. Her voice was pushed to the edge of tears. She looked at them both accusingly.

Raven retrieved the envelope from the ground. It was addressed to Barbara Beattie at Lamprecht's house in Chelsea.

'It's what you said, isn't it?' she asked aggressively. 'Suicide. He's going to kill himself.'

He scratched the top of his scalp, frowning. 'No,' he said at length. 'No, I don't think so. You don't find a secret hideaway to do yourself in. You can do that anywhere.'

She winced, but she was unrepentant. The sooner they came down to earth the better.

Zaleski came in with forthright approval. 'Precisely. Now, what we are doing is . . .'

Raven held up a hand. 'Not now, Casimir. Please!' He took a turn as far as the french windows. A foot had flattened on one of the molehills that dotted the lawn beyond the verandah. He could just see the heads and arms of the couple next door. They were hanging Chinese lanterns against the walls. Lamprecht's behaviour made it unlikely that they'd even know that he was in the house. He turned to Barbara.

'We're going to search the place thoroughly. Anything

49

we find that could be connected with Lamprecht goes on here.' He tapped the top of the grand piano. Zaleski and the girl followed him out into the corridor. He sent the Pole left.

'Try the kitchen. You're looking for scraps of paper, cigarette ends, anything. You take the nursery and bathroom,' he instructed the girl.

He went through the dining room, checking the drawers in the dark massive sideboard. He stood in the doorway of the main bedroom, tall and gangling, like a heron scanning marsh water for the faintest sign of movement. The mattress on one of the beds was down on one side as if someone had been sitting on it. He lowered himself into the depression, staring at the worn red carpet. A glint of metal caught his eye and then another. He picked up three short pieces of single-strand wire, the last close to a power socket. The wire was plastic-coated and copper, the sort of thing used on a radio. A few cigarette ends in an ashtray were the only other objects that could have been connected with Lamprecht. The others were waiting for him in the drawing room. Zaleski cleared his throat and shook his head from side to side.

'Nothing. Cupboards are empty. Not even a bloody beer.'

'What cigarettes does he smoke, Barbara?' demanded Raven. The brand matched those in the bedroom.

The girl looked at him nervously, indicating the razor, toothbrush and sponge bag.

'That's all I could find.' She seemed to be waiting for some sort of miracle, a sign that only he could interpret.

He tipped out the contents of the sponge bag. A clip of razor blades, a piece of soap and a small phial of bright blue pills. The chemist's wrapper identified the contents.

MORPANIL 10mg
1-2 four times a day or as needed. Mr. Lamprecht.
D. Macauley M.P.S.
Fulham Road, S.W.10
Tel. 01-373 00491

He weighed the tiny bottle in the palm of his hand, looking at Barbara.

'*Now* at last we're getting somewhere.'

She lit a cigarette with nervous fingers. Every movement she made, everything she said, was produced with a kind of uncontrollable energy.

'You mean we can find out what medicine Henryk is taking?'

'Better yet, we can find who his doctor is,' he answered. He lifted the receiver on the side table. The 'phone was still connected. He held up a warning finger and dialled. A man's voice answered.

'Macauley's, Fulham Road.'

'Good morning,' Raven said smoothly. 'My name is Lamprecht. Look, I wonder if you could help me. It's about my Morpanil. I have to ask for a renewal and I'm not quite sure who prescribed it. Was it Doctor Horton or not?'

'I didn't quite get your name,' said the voice. 'Would you mind spelling it, please. Just a minute and I'll check for you.'

Raven waited, holding his hand over the mouthpiece from habit. The other two watched in silence, cigarette smoke curling in front of Barbara Beattie's troubled face, Zaleski's pose judicious as if he knew what was going on but wasn't prepared to commit himself.

'There must be some mistake,' the chemist's voice was

doubtful. 'According to our records you collected two bottles of Morpanil the day before yesterday. That's one hundred tablets.'

'This is the problem,' Raven said quickly. 'I seem to have lost them on the way home.'

There was a short silence before the chemist answered. 'Have you reported the loss to the police?' Raven hesitated. 'You'll have to, you know,' the man added. 'These things are on the Dangerous Drugs List. There'll be hell to pay if they get into the hands of the wrong people. Children or someone.'

'I'll do it right away,' promised Raven. 'But in the meantime I need a renewal.'

The doubtful tone hardened to one of frank suspicion. 'Then you'll have to get another prescription from Doctor Belling. I can't let you have any more pills without it, I'm afraid.'

Raven replaced the receiver very gently. The telephone books were out-of-date but he took the buff A–D volume and squatted on the floor. He was feeling better-tempered than he had been for the last three or four hours. It was good to recapture the initiative or at least act as if he'd recaptured it. There were only three Bellings listed as doctors. One was in Greenwich, another in Hampstead, the third in Chelsea.

Dr. Raymond Belling M.D.

39 Cadnam Street

S.W.3

He looked at his watch. It was almost one o'clock. He spun the dial with a forefinger and a girl came on the line.

'Dr. Belling's surgery, good afternoon.'

Raven's voice and manner were business-like. 'This is Macauley's of Fulham Road. We have a prescription here for a Mr. Lamprecht. Morpanil. Would that be 10mg or 20? We can't decipher the doctor's figures.'

'One moment,' she said swiftly. The sound of her voice filtered through as she spoke to someone else in the room. 'It's 10mg. T-e-n. All right?'

'Thanks very much.' He put the phone down and glanced up at Barbara from where he sat on the floor. 'Dr. Belling. Cadnam Street. That's at the bottom of Oakley Street.'

She wiped her mouth with the back of her hand as if she didn't understand.

'You think I could go to him and explain?'

'Explain about what?' he demanded. 'We're looking for explanations not giving them.' He climbed up, dusting off the seat of his jeans. She was far less sure than she had been and he wanted her to admire his resourcefulness. He no longer had any feeling of guilt. What was left was a mixture of excitement and the wish to impress.

'Look, let me handle this,' he said. 'We don't have much chance anyway. Doctors don't talk about their patients. I can but try. In the meantime you stay here in case Lamprecht does show up.'

She gave him her slow reluctant smile. 'You sure try to make amends. I'll say that for you. Don't worry, I'll be all right.'

'You stay with her,' he said to Zaleski. 'And if and when he comes get down on your bended knees and apologize.'

Zaleski's eyebrows rose. 'Is nice idea but for Poles is no defeat or apologies. *Bloody* apologies,' he amended.

Raven shrugged. 'Then just disappear. I'll be back as

53

soon as I can. If the 'phone rings twice and then stops, the next time pick it up. It'll be me. Otherwise stay away from it altogether.'

Zaleski let him out through the back door. He arrived in Chelsea in time to see a woman locking a door at the top of the steps. He swung in to the kerb, parked and stuck his head out of the window.

'I say there, just a minute, please!'

She turned, standing under the black-and-orange awning, clutching her handbag close to her chest as he loped across the street. He reached the pavement at the same moment as she did, appearing to cut her off as she headed for a nearby Volkswagen.

'Dr. Belling's surgery?' he asked politely.

She was in her early forties and apprehensive. 'That's right, yes, but the doctor left twenty minutes ago. Surgery hours are from ten to one.'

The two-storey house was smaller than its neighbours and by the look of things used only as business premises. The four brass plates indicated a partnership practice. It was broad daylight and they were only a few yards from Oakley Street but she stared anxiously over his shoulder.

'Do you know where I could get hold of the doctor?' He offered a placatory smile. 'It's about one of his patients.'

Pale blue eyes flashed behind her thin-rimmed spectacles. 'One of our patients?'

'Mr. Henryk Lamprecht.' He produced the name easily, stepping aside as she moved towards the small blue car determinedly.

She turned behind a defensive shoulder, plucking the ignition keys from her handbag.

'Didn't you call about half-an-hour ago? Are you something to do with Macauley's, the chemist's?'

'Nothing,' he said, opening the car door for her. 'It's a personal matter and one the doctor ought to know about.'

The motor clattered to life. She drove in string-and-leather gloves in spite of the heat.

'You could try Paultons Square but I don't know if he'll be there. The number is 314.'

CHAPTER FIVE

Lamprecht, Wednesday

He went by Underground as far as Victoria and bought a ticket for a cinema, dozing in the air-conditioned theatre. The voices on the screen mingled with those from the past. His daughter's laugh seemed to sound as she ran to meet him on some beach, her arms spread wide. He woke with a start and wiped the hot tears from his eyes. It was twenty to four when he left the theatre and made his way along Petty France to a short street running towards St. James's Park. Most of the houses had been taken over by architects. Men were working at drawing boards inside open sunny windows. The corner edifice was in contrast to the eighteenth-century elegance, a six-storey building with the starkness of an armoury. The tennis courts on the flat roof were surrounded by a tall wire fence that partly hid the forest of radio antennas. A flight of stone steps led up to heavy doors under a porch. The brass plate on the wall read:

CROWN DEVELOPMENT BOARD
(Interviews by appointment only)

Lamprecht inserted the punched plastic card in the slit lock, presenting himself to the scanner which would identify him and record the time of his entry. The door opened and closed automatically. A uniformed sergeant threw a vague salute. He was wearing a heavy-calibre service pistol in a holster and the insignia of the Special Air Services Regiment.

'Afternoon, Mr. Lamprecht.'

The two lower floors in the building were open-plan offices and staffed by civilians. Lamprecht made his way to the lifts. The one on the right was marked *Express*. He used his card again to open the doors and went to the fifth floor. The corridor was painted in eggshell-white enamel, its institutional appearance exaggerated by cork-lined doors and windows made of opaque glass. The lights burned summer and winter. He pushed open the door of the changing room. Inside was an array of lavatories and wash basins, a few showers. He stripped down to his underwear, exchanging his own clothes and shoes for the freshly-laundered overalls and felt slippers in his locker. Nothing personal, not even a ring or watch, was allowed beyond the checkpoint. Cigarettes, matches and soft drinks were provided. He pressed a button. The television camera flickered an image and Lamprecht stepped through the metal-detector screen. The second S.A.S. security guard had ginger hair and a sun-peeled nose. He was sitting at a folding card-table, his service revolver in front of him. He looked across at the electric wall-clock and grinned.

'There's got to be some mistake. You and Mr. Burke early on the same day. It doesn't make sense.'

Six insulated offices opened onto a high-ceilinged corridor controlled by television cameras. There was no sound between ceiling and wall-to-wall carpet. It was as quiet as a church. Each of the five sections had its own sphere for deciphering foreign communications. The monitoring itself was done up on the sixth, the messages recorded and typed and passed down for processing. It was almost four o'clock by the hands on the wall. A door opened and Stashinsky came out to the water-cooler. He was a squat beetfaced Ukrainian who doodled drawings of horses galloping across the steppes. An orderly emptied the wastepaper baskets for incineration after each tour of duty, but Lamprecht had seen the impressions on the scribbling-pad.

Stashinsky drank noisily, wiped the back of his hand across his mouth and offered a clenched-fist salute. He spoke in Russian.

'Greetings, Comrade! Power to the people!'

Lamprecht frowned. The Ukrainian's humour was heavy, bucolic and abrasive. Lamprecht answered in English.

'How much have you left in the tray?'

Stashinsky belched. The front of his overalls was mysteriously streaked with what appeared to be egg. He blinked with bright blue eyes, seemingly on the point of some confidence when his red peasant's face grew cunning.

'Everything is in order, Excellency. All is well in the Russian sector.'

Lamprecht closed the door on him. The layout of the spacious room was designed for the inmate's comfort. Pale green walls rested the eyes, the long mirror was reassuring. The atmosphere was always sixty-five degrees Fahrenheit with the correct amount of humidity. It could be winter outside, the room would never reveal it. A metal chute descended from ceiling to desk. The cypher messages came down from the sixth floor, recorded and typed automatically on blue flimsy paper. There was an angle lamp with a dimming device, a red housephone with six buzzers, pencils and felt-tipped pens, codebooks bound like film-scripts. Each was stamped TOP SECRET.

In the centre of the desk was the decoding machine, twice as large as the model Lamprecht had made and a computerized version of Goering's wartime ENIGMA. Its familiar name was Ghost.

He sat down, adjusting the height and tilt of the chair till he was sitting in his favourite position. The cigarette box had been refilled. Stashinsky smoked cigars. Half-an-hour went by before a plastic tube came down the chute. He unrolled the two sheets and clipped them on the easel in front of him. The message was timed sixteen hours forty and bore the call-sign of a K.G.B. communication centre. He stared at it through narrowed eyes, cigarette smoke clouding the side of his face. The Russian text was garbled. He punched the message out on the decoding machine in front of him, the result acquiring sudden clarity like dotted letters on a colour chart. He picked up a pen and transcribed. The message was simple: the Soviet Embassy in Prague requesting some routine information from their Paris counterpart. He wrote in Cyrillic script then translated, using the electric typewriter. He shoved the finished work in a manilla envelope, scribbled his initials on it and threw the envelope in the OUT tray. A Duty Orderly collected the contents of the trays at the end of each shift and removed them to the Director's office. There was nothing in what he'd just read to warrant the use of the 'phone.

Time went slowly, the silence only occasionally broken by the rattle of containers in the chute, the clatter of his typewriter. It was a day of unimportant communications, some of them in plain: raw reports of happenings abroad on their way to Moscow for official interpretation. He

worked mechanically, his mind leaping ahead to his plan
for tomorrow, his body stiff like a dog that sees a rabbit.
He had no fear any more of death, the Pale Sweetheart as
someone had called it. His only fear was of failure. It was
well after seven when he went to the water-cooler. The
security guard on the door had been changed. An unfamiliar face greeted Lamprecht's appearance with surly
suspicion. He filled his dry mouth with water and spat the
flat tasteless liquid into the bowl. Suddenly he turned,
sensing someone standing close behind him. It was Burke,
in the uniform overalls, prematurely bald with reptilian
eyes and a rim of indigestion powder round the edges of
his lips. His voice was twenty years older than the rest of
him, a sort of bray produced entirely through his nose.

'Henryk, old man. I'm glad I caught you in time. I
wanted a word with you.'

Apprehension tightened Lamprecht's stomach. His fingers flew to the side of his head unconsciously.

'A word about what?'

Burke's glance found the security guard. He wrapped a
protective arm about Lamprecht's shoulders, his breath
smelling of bismuth.

'Let's go into my place, it's cosier.'

It was an odd description for a room that was identical
with Lamprecht's. Security Officers were chosen from the
native-born Britons on the establishment. Burke worked
in the Centre full-time. His specialities were Italian and
Romanian. He pushed the only chair in Lamprecht's direction and offered a packet of cigarettes. Lamprecht shook
his head guardedly.

'Can we get this over quickly? I have to clear my desk.'

Burke smiled narrowly. 'You think of nothing but duty,

do you, Henryk? We've time. I suppose you know what I'm going to say.'

The blinding pain was back, twisting Lamprecht's optic nerves and roaring in his eardrums. He forced his face and voice to conceal it.

'I have no idea,' he said clearly.

Burke perched on the edge of the desk almost coyly. 'We're worried about you, Henryk. You haven't been yourself for some time. I'm talking about those dizzy spells.'

The tick of the clock was distinct, a remorseless reminder of dwindling time. A week had passed since he'd had the attack in the changing room, shortly after he'd deciphered the message from Ankara. It was in a new code, one that the Russians hadn't used before, based on the diatonic scale of F sharp. It had taken him two hours with Ghost to break it.

He'd read the short message through with shocked incredulity.

HURRICANE FLYING TO LONDON JUNE FIFTEENTH STOP PROVIDE TRANSPORT FROM AIRPORT AND EMBASSY LODGING STOP ADDITIONAL INFORMATION FORWARDED IN DIPLOMATIC BAG

His wife's murderer had changed names and pseudonyms over the years but the mark of the beast was on him. Lamprecht had followed each mutation, tracking them through the waste of gossip and rumour with relentless purpose. And now he had it. *For Hurricane read Butov.* He had destroyed the original text, the code notes, substituting some innocuous message. The next thing he re-

membered was being found in the changing rooms by
Burke, lying half-conscious across the wash basins.

Lamprecht glanced up. 'There's nothing to worry about.
I saw my doctor. He gave me some tests and said it was
blood-pressure. Too much work.' He attempted a grin that
failed.

'Who *is* your doctor?' asked Burke, his head on one
side.

Lamprecht's brain shied violently and invented a name.
'You wouldn't have heard of him. He's Polish.'

'That's *precisely* what we thought,' Burke said behind
a pointing finger. 'You need a proper opinion.'

The slur was careless but almost certainly intentional.
Lamprecht's hands tightened into fists, his nails digging
into his palms.

'I'm perfectly satisfied with the one I have. And that's
the second time you've used the pronoun "we". Is there
somebody else involved?'

Burke's eyes were unblinking. 'The Department,
Henryk. Let's see, how long is it that you've been with
us now?'

'Seventeen years.'

The memory of his arrival in England flickered and
grew. From Poland to Russia to Poland and Hungary, the
dream had always been of the west. From the west came
freedom and this had been his first glimpse of it. They
had separated him from the others as he walked off the
boat at Dover. Quiet-voiced men speaking his own language had taken him into the Immigration building and
fed him cups of tea and ham sandwiches. He'd slept on a
bunk, the dream fading as the interrogation continued.
Suddenly he'd been provided with new clothes and driven
to London where strangers had asked more questions till

his life held no more secrets. They'd given him a new name and a room in a house in Hampstead. For the next year he'd gone to the Code and Cypher School, obeying the instructions of his new protectors and meeting each test of his loyalty with dogged determination. They were shrewdly conceived and continuous, culminating in the scene staged on Hampstead Heath. The girl had been Polish and desirable, daughter of a couple who'd escaped from Warsaw during the uprising. He'd slept in her bed surrendering nothing in return. The following week he'd taken the oath under the Official Secrets Act and started work in the Centre. The Department had financed his cover occupation. Hard work had made the translation bureau prosper. He had played the rules that the British had written offering loyal service. And now the game was over.

'Seventeen years,' he repeated. 'Longer than you have.'

Burke's wolfish teeth crunched hungrily on an indigestion tablet. 'That's why we have to take care of you, Henryk. The Department *needs* people of your calibre. The Director has arranged for you to see a specialist. Ten a.m. next Tuesday. King Edward VII's Hospital for Officers. Just give your name at Reception, they'll be expecting you.' He slid from his perch, opened the door and looked back at the clock. 'It's only twenty to eight, you see. Plenty of time to clear your desk. There's no question of you coming back on duty till after you've had your check-up. You realize that, of course.'

'Of course.' Lamprecht forced himself to smile again. 'You'll find that even a Polish doctor can be right.'

He crossed the silent corridor to his own office and sat down heavily, weak with relief. To be suspected for the right cause and wrong reason, that was ironical.

He put his desk in order. There was nothing more in the chute. Fifteen minutes to go. He shifted the red 'phone with its bank of call-buttons. There'd be no more messages, no more letters. The last act would be both epitaph and explanation. It was exactly one minute past eight as he passed through the metal-detector screen for the last time.

CHAPTER SIX

Thoroughgood, Wednesday

George Thoroughgood's fifth-floor room was the same as the others except for the furnishings. The rolltop desk and easy chairs had been brought from university, the *chaise-longue* he had found in a Notting Hill salesroom together with the print of Landseer's *Monarch of the Glen*. Painter and treatment were unfashionably sentimental but he found something splendid in the stag's majestic defiance. He was made on the short side, a man in his early sixties reminiscent in appearance of the late Rudyard Kipling with a grizzled frieze surrounding a sunburned pate and half-spectacles worn on the end of his fleshy nose. He was dressed in an old suit of mustard-coloured tweed, a flannel shirt and a bright orange silk tie given to him by his younger daughter.

Four television screens were bracketed on the wall in front of him. The screen on the right showed Lamprecht leaving the building by the front entrance, an erect figure with short stiff white hair and a wide Tartar face. He was walking quickly looking neither left nor right till the camera lost him. Thoroughgood's fingers found the fluff in his right ear. A plain van appeared on the screen moving slowly in the direction Lamprecht had taken. Thoroughgood was unable to see the driver's seat but he could guess who would occupy it. A man, possibly a woman, inconspicuous, while in the back of the van would be two more people with a bicycle or motorcycle. The trio would keep Lamprecht under surveillance till another crew took over. And so on, night and day, till the order was signed that would call them off.

The thought of one of his own men under suspicion offended him. It was a slur on his judgement that he resented. It was all Burke's fault, of course. Burke the renegade monk with the brain of a Jesuit and the nose of a weasel. Twenty years in some bloody monastery had left the fellow with no interest other than plot and counterplot, a busybody who spent his time looking for Pandora's boxes he might open. He took the monthly stint as Security Officer so seriously. Everyone working in the place had been vetted by at least three different boards. They were men of dedication and honour. But Burke seemed to spend his time listening at privy keyholes. If you did that for long enough you were bound to hear something unpleasant.

Thoroughgood shifted his fingers from his right ear to a button on his desk. Someone rapped on the door almost immediately. Burke came in bouncing on the balls of his feet, flat-eyed above his sharp questing nose.

'You wanted me, Director?'

Thoroughgood pushed a chair with his foot. There was no love lost between them and neither made too much effort to hide the fact.

'For crissakes sit down, Burke. You make me nervous prancing around like that. You spoke to Lamprecht?'

'I did,' Burke said shortly. He switched his gaze to the television screens and hopped it from one to another. 'I said we were concerned about the state of his health and that you'd made arrangements for him to go to King Edward's on Tuesday.'

Thoroughgood pulled a gold watch from his fob-pocket. The quarter-hour chimed as he looked at the Roman numerals. It was seventy years old and still keeping better time than this electrical monstrosity on the desk.

'What was his reaction?'

Burke's shoulders rose and fell. 'Surprise. Surprise and apprehension. He said that he'd already been to see a doctor. I gathered some Pole. The man's supposed to have told him that the dizzy spells are nothing more than high blood pressure. Or low. I can't remember which. I intimated that you'd be having a chat with him yourself after Tuesday.'

The Director explored the jagged edge of a broken wisdom-tooth. His avoidance of Lamprecht had been deliberate. His sympathies were already engaged and a face-to-face meeting with the Pole might have further impaired his judgement.

'Well, that's that, then, Burke. You've done your job. As far as you're concerned that's the end of this affair. Thank you.'

Burke's tongue darted out, licking the dried powder from the edge of his mouth.

'There *is* something else . . .'

The Director's sigh was unconscious. 'What?'

'I've been feeding him placebos all evening.'

Thoroughgood leaned forward incredulously. 'You've been feeding him *what*?'

The words came with a rush. 'Dummy messages, sir. I

have them here.' He pulled a bunch of blue flimsies from his overall pocket. 'Stashinsky prepared them. He didn't know what he was doing, of course. I told him they were needed at the School for instructional purposes.'

Thoroughgood looked at the papers with distaste. 'And?'

Burke's smile lost its confidence. 'Lamprecht transcribed them correctly.'

'What did you expect him to do?' demanded Thoroughgood.

Burke hesitated, his eyes between his feet. 'Exactly what he did, I suppose,' he said, looking up. 'If my hunch is right the damage has already been done.'

'And what damage does your hunch say it is?' Thoroughgood asked sarcastically.

'I don't know, sir,' Burke admitted. 'I'm just certain that something happened that afternoon. He was mumbling when I found him in the changing room – he couldn't even stand straight. When I got him up, his eyes were completely out of focus. But he did say one word. A word I remembered and that Stashinsky translated. It's the Russian for "hurricane" and it doesn't appear in his work for that day.'

'Nor do twenty thousand others in his vocabulary,' the Director said drily. 'We deal in facts in this Department, Burke, not hunches. That'll be all.' He let the other man near the door. 'And incidentally!'

Burke turned quickly, his face expectant. 'Sir?'

'Wipe that disgusting mess from your mouth.'

The door closed quietly. Thoroughgood let his breath go, annoyed at himself for the outburst, at Burke for provoking it. The truth was, he needed a holiday. But August with the still clear water of Loch Morsgail and the pine

forest behind seemed all too far away. He stuffed the sheaf
of blue paper into a drawer and locked his desk. The
last shift of the day was at work behind closed doors. His
deputy would still be in the changing room. It was
Venables who, with Burke, was responsible for this whole
unpleasant affair. Venables who had franked Burke's
original report elevating it to a status where there had been
nothing left but to call in S Department. The security
guard came to his feet seeing Thoroughgood. He switched
off the metal-detector, allowing the Director to go through
the screen to the elevator. A second guard repeated the
process on the sixth floor. It was much noisier up here
with half-open doors offering glimpses of rooms where
men with headphones worked at shortwave radio sets.
Static crackled from the masts on the roof. Eyes glowed
on facia boards and a generator droned monotonously.

Thoroughgood knocked on a door marked NO ENTRY.
The man who opened it was wearing an open-necked silk
shirt, faded jeans and Spanish riding boots. He was sharp-
featured with long side-whiskers and a Fu Manchu
moustache. Something about his bearing suggested a military training. Thoroughgood was prepared to accept it as
fact. They were all of the same breed, social misfits.
Cashiered service officers, ex-convicts and psychopaths, the
troubled in spirit with an itch for excitement. He disliked
the concept of the Dirty Tricks Department intensely.
Expediency was one thing, a complete denial of process
of law another. These people committed crime under the
blanket of the Defence of the Realm Act and Orders in
Council.

The man stuck his hand out, offering a firm light grip.
'I'm Slade, Director. We talked on the telephone yesterday. I'm in charge of this investigation.'

There was a touch of Eton about his educated voice, a slight arrogance of manner. Thoroughgood put a couple of feet between them.

'How do you do?'

There was nothing in the room but a couple of chairs, a white screen against the wall and a projector. Slade lit a long brown-papered cigarette.

'There are a few questions I have to ask you, Director, before we run these frames. I hope you'll bear with me.'

'Ask away,' answered Thoroughgood.

Slade shifted his weight from one leg to the other. His jeans were frayed at the bottoms but the cuffs of his shirt were clipped with crested gold.

'These cameras you have downstairs. I understand there are five. My information is that they're completely concealed?'

Thoroughgood removed his spectacles and rubbed the weal they had left on his nose.

'You people fitted them.'

Slade showed good teeth in an easy smile. The moustache gave him a slightly sardonic expression.

'It comes to us all, I'm afraid. The Kaska affair wasn't exactly good publicity.'

The desire to wrench Slade's head from his shoulders was strong. Thoroughgood moved out of range of the sweet-smelling tobacco smoke. Kaska had never actually been in the Department. A Czech defector with homosexual tendencies, he'd been turned round and detected while still at the Code and Cypher School. The cameras had been installed in the Centre the following month.

'I understand that they're concealed behind mirrors,' the Director said icily. 'I haven't inspected the locations myself.'

'Of course not,' Slade said soothingly. His eyebrows winged together. He consulted a piece of paper and read from it. 'Nikon two-fifty exposure backs with motor drives and radio remote control. The control would be up here, I suppose?'

'The control is in my desk,' the Director said stiffly.

Slade's smile was understanding. 'I should have guessed. Now what else have we got? F. 2.8 lens, exposure 1/60th at F. 4 which is supposed to mean that anything that moves in the room is stopped in focus. I'm told that banks use them,' he added conversationally.

'Riveting,' said Thoroughgood.

It seemed that Slade was a hard man to rile. He flicked ash at the carpet.

'How many people in the building know that these cameras exist?'

The Director disliked him more with each question. 'Three. Myself and my two deputies. You can take it for granted that we've been discreet.'

Slade's wave of the hand was deferent. 'So we know how we stand. The film goes to the Signal Corps for developing and is monitored by you, correct? How often is this done, Director?'

'Every Friday evening,' said Thoroughgood. 'And it's the longest, most useless bloody boring hour in the week. On a par with supervising the shredding machine.'

Slade's eyes were keen. 'I was going to ask about that. Is any of the film shredded or do you keep it all?'

'We keep it all,' Thoroughgood said distinctly. 'Every single inch of it. There's a room in the basement that houses the archives. You're free to inspect it, if you wish.'

'That won't be necessary,' Slade replied. 'Look, sir, I can understand your feelings about all this but it is our job.' He stationed himself behind the projector, the pose revealing two-inch heels on the boots he was wearing. 'Shall we roll this film?' he asked quietly.

He turned off the lights. Thoroughgood seated himself on the left. The projector whirred in the darkness. The screen became the interior of Lamprecht's office, seen from the mirror facing the desk. The pictures were clear, the pattern of the Pole's brogues, the double crown in his brush of white hair, the nervous movements of his fingers. It was the first time Thoroughgood had noticed that the Pole wore a wedding ring on his right hand. Lamprecht was going through the movements of a man who thinks himself alone, tapping a cigarette on the desk, yawning, staring vacantly at the wall. Occasionally he touched his left eye and temple as though in pain. A cylinder slid down the chute and he reached for it. He removed the blue paper inside.

The projection room was silent except for the noise of the machine. Lamprecht stretched and punched the keys of the decoder in front of him. He stared at the end result as if dumbfounded, his head cocked on one side. He held the pose for fully three minutes before shoving his chair back brusquely. The image froze as he stopped the machine. His voice was cool and impersonal.

'Is he alarmed, intrigued or what? Here's a man who's spent – what is it? – fifteen years decoding monitored material. Yet suddenly he's looking as though he's stumbled on a new version of the Gospels. Odd when you remember that there's absolutely nothing in the text he turned in that would account for his behaviour.'

Thoroughgood made no reply. He had seen the film four times before S Department had taken it away and he'd had the same reaction on each occasion.

'And so on,' Slade said easily, running the next few frames at high speed. He slowed again to normal speed. 'Seven minutes later.' The film showed Lamprecht blocking something out on the pad in front of him, lips moving. His face seemed to crumple as he wrote till he looked shocked and sick. He sat for a while and then started to write again till the top of the desk was littered with crumpled pieces of paper. He collected these, burned them in the ashtray and rubbed the ashes into the carpet with the sole of his slipper.

A few more minutes elapsed then he used the electric typewriter, glancing from the machine to the note he had made. Finished, he stapled the two sheets together and initialled the envelope.

Slade's smile mocked Thoroughgood in the sudden blaze of light. 'There's nothing in that last sequence that you find odd, Director?'

Thoroughgood rose and stretched arms and legs one after another. 'If by "odd" you mean sinister, no. If you mean out-of-the-ordinary, yes.'

Slade unwound the film from the sprockets and put it back in the can.

'I've seen four films of Lamprecht in addition to this one. They cover the period since the cameras were installed and were chosen at random. Only once is he seen to burn his notes. You don't appear to like the word "odd". How about "suspicious"?'

Thoroughgood shrugged. He was getting too old for this sort of thing. He could have – probably should have – called Lamprecht in and given the Pole the chance to provide an explanation. Events had overtaken him.

'Suspicious, perhaps,' he agreed reluctantly.

Slade's face brightened. 'We're agreed on something,

good. I keep asking myself why Lamprecht destroyed what he'd written that day and that day alone. Records show he deciphered every message sent down to him. The monitor time-stamps narrow the field to one piece of work. I'm saying that Lamprecht substituted some routine piece of nonsense and kept quiet about the real text. Without the Poles, remember, Jerzy Rozycki and the other mathematicians, you wouldn't have Ghost.'

'You seem to have researched your subject.' Thoroughgood's face was wry.

Slade winked. 'It's a habit and Lamprecht's a Pole.'

Thoroughgood blinked. 'I'm not sure that I understand. Are you suggesting that Lamprecht's in touch with Warsaw?'

'Are you suggesting that he's not?' Slade's moustached grin widened the lower half of his face.

His easy manner had hardened. He was the inquisitor now and Thoroughgood resented it.

'You haven't thought of an alternative explanation?'

Slade shook his head. 'I've no time to waste.'

'He's a sick man, under strain,' said Thoroughgood. 'You only have to look at that film to see it. Half-an-hour after that was taken he collapsed in the changing room.'

'Exactly.' Slade took a turn to the wall and back. 'This chap who found him, the Security Officer, Burke. Does he have any idea that the rooms are visually monitored?'

It was increasingly difficult for Thoroughgood to control his temper.

'I've already answered that. There are only three people in this building who know. My two deputies and myself.' He consulted his watch. It was a quarter to nine, too late now to eat at home. Both his daughters would be out and he had no heart to search a refrigerator.

Slade hitched his jeans up. 'Is Burke still in the building?'

Thoroughgood shook his head.

'Then I'd like you to arrange for him to see me,' said Slade. 'Send him down to Priory Park tomorrow morning. If that's convenient, of course.' His eyes were very bright.

Thoroughgood wasted a smile. 'He'll like that. You'll find him a willing subject. He's given to hunches and he doesn't approve of Lamprecht.'

'And I take it you do?' Slade's smile was supposed to take the sting from his words.

The Director summoned the last of his patience. 'I'm a scholar, Mr. Slade, not a policeman. A man with a record like Lamprecht's is entitled to my trust until such time as he forfeits it. I don't want to sound discourteous, but it's late and I'm hungry. Let me see you out of the building.'

Someone rapped on the door. The duty-sergeant flashed a salute at Thoroughgood.

'A telephone call for the gentleman, sir.'

Slade was back in a couple of minutes, his face thoughtful. 'I wouldn't be too confident if I were you. Your man's just given us the slip. Walked into a church, crossed himself and disappeared. I'm going after the bugger myself.'

It was a word that Thoroughgood had always disliked. 'I still find it incredible,' he said.

'Not me,' said Slade. He combed his moustache with a forefinger. 'Lamprecht lives in Chelsea, doesn't he?'

'Justice Place.'

'I'll need his file,' said Slade. 'With any sort of luck we'll have him down in the country before morning. Give me a ring there. There are two Slades, incidentally. I'm Sebastian.'

They rode down in silence, parting outside the front

entrance. The street stood empty in the warmth of the summer evening. Slade offered his brief warm grasp.

'I'm sorry if I've rubbed you the wrong way, Director. It happens too frequently. But then we don't expect to make friends in our business.'

CHAPTER SEVEN

Thoroughgood, Wednesday

Thoroughgood collected his yellowed panama hat and walking stick from the downstairs hall and walked slowly in the direction of St. James's Park. He was in no mood for the club where he still passed as a lecturer in Comparative Literature. But at least they'd give him scrambled eggs or something. The park was still full, couples strolling arm-in-arm in the fading light. The young made love openly under the trees where starlings chattered and squabbled.

Slade was much on his mind. A disturbing breed, ruthless and unpitying, defenders of a faith they secretly doubted. A man like Slade would kill without remorse and there were many more like him at Priory Park. Thoroughgood had been there on one occasion, an occasion he tried to forget. The hamlet huddled in a fold of the Marlborough Downs. It was a place of peace and grey stone houses, where stableyards opened onto twisting leafy lanes. Racehorses had been climbing the hill on their way to early morning exercise as he arrived from London. The hideous Victorian mansion was a couple of miles from the village, set in three hundred acres of ancient oak and chestnut trees. The woods were festooned with electronic devices. A board outside the lodge gates proclaimed the estate to be

POLYURETHANE PRODUCTS LTD.
Experimental Station

A second board added the warning:

BEWARE! GUARD DOGS PATROLLING!

A curious mind searching the Companies Register would find the parent company listed as Polyurethane Products A.G. with an address in Vaduz, Liechtenstein. Inquirers there were referred to Curaçao and the office of a Goanese lawyer who was always elsewhere. The men behind the creeper-covered walls and fake gables operated beyond the law, protected by the stonewall provisions of the Defence of the Realm Act and innumerable Orders in Council. The Interrogation Centre was at the back of the house, the walls of the isolation room smooth and unbroken, the door set flush. Nothing disturbed the sweep of the eye. The small high window was protected by three sets of steel bars. A plastic screen let in the light while denying the occupant the smallest sight of the world outside. A forty-watt bulb burned in the ceiling. There was a chair in the room and nothing else. Something happened to the men who were questioned in there. They never came out the same. The so-called resident psychiatrist had been blandly reassuring to Thoroughgood. Physical cruelty? There was no need for it. 'Sensory deprivation' broke down the strongest resistance. The memory of the man Thoroughgood had seen there was etched in his brain, a drooping dull-eyed creature with days' stubble on his face. The psychiatrist had stood in front of him, gentle and reasonable, setting him up for the others who stood behind, terriers waiting to go in for the kill.

It had taken Thoroughgood some time to get his objections on paper. He still remembered the gist. What he had seen had been 'an erosion of Human Rights'. The envelope was still in his desk, the rolltop desk that had come with him from Cambridge, sullied now with its drawers harbouring records of doubt and suspicion. He climbed the steps of the dirty stone building. The lights were on in the library, men hidden in the high-winged leather armchairs. The porter took Thoroughgood's hat and stick.

'It's been a lovely day, Professor. A really lovely day.'

'A lovely day,' echoed Thoroughgood. The dining room doors were shut but he could see his favourite waiter.

CHAPTER EIGHT

Raven and Zaleski, Wednesday

A man was eating behind the dining room windows. Raven rang the door bell but nobody answered. He rang again. This time the door was partially opened by a small dark woman dressed in maid's uniform.

She achieved a degree of suspicion in the question. 'Yes, please?'

'Dr. Belling?' He was aware that she was inspecting his sneakers and jeans with disapproval.

'Doctor eating,' she snapped.

He held the closing door with his shoulder. 'Tell him

there's someone here to see him. It's important.'

The gap widened in the door. He saw that it was made by the man he had seen eating, a well-built man in his forties with thick rope-coloured hair and eyebrows. He was in his shirt-sleeves and without a tie.

'That's all right, Fidelia,' he said pleasantly. 'I'll see to this. Yes?' he added to Raven.

'If I could see you for a moment,' Raven said quickly. 'It's about Henryk Lamprecht. My name's John Raven.'

Belling's eyes were bright blue and piercingly direct. 'Come on in,' he invited and shut the door after Raven.

They were standing in a hallway that was panelled in polished pine like the staircase. Beyond a door at the end steps led down to grass growing beneath a giant mulberry tree.

'Why not let me wait somewhere while you finish your meal?' suggested Raven.

Belling's face was cheerful. 'I don't think we'll worry about that. They don't know it downstairs apparently, but baked fish and tomatoes isn't my favourite dish. Let's go outside.'

He led the way down the steps to deckchairs set in the spread of the mulberry tree. Croquet hoops spiked the lawn on the other side and a mallet was leaning against a stone bust covered with bird-droppings. Belling shifted one of the chairs in Raven's direction.

'Sit yourself down,' he invited. 'Now what's all this about Henryk Lamprecht?'

Raven crossed long legs. The doctor's friendly appearance and manner invited frankness, but Raven was cautious. There was far more in this whole thing than a man running from a drunken accusation. The taking of the riverside house, the letter Lamprecht had written were parts of a deliberate plan. And somewhere in it was a place for the newly-cut pieces of wire he had found. He was sure of it and reminded himself to search the bedroom again.

'Do you smoke, Mr. Raven?' Belling was holding up a silver cigarette case.

Raven produced his own crumpled blue package. 'I don't know how much you know of Lamprecht's personal life, Doctor, but there's a crisis going on. He's more or less been living with a Canadian girl who's very much in love with him.'

Belling leaned back, closed his eyes and blew a perfect smoke ring.

'I think we'd better establish your role first, don't you?'

An over-ripe mulberry plopped on his shirt sleeve. He opened his eyes and brushed at the purple stain. Raven considered the toes of his sneakers.

'I've never even spoken to the man. In fact I saw him last night for the first time in my life. If you'd like to check just who I am, call Detective-Inspector Soo at Scotland Yard.'

'A policeman?' Belling tilted his head.

'Was,' corrected Raven. 'I'm involved in this purely by accident. Lamprecht walked out of his house in the early hours of this morning leaving the girl in his bed. She's asked me to help her find him. It's as simple as that.'

Belling's smile was genial. 'You seem to have an odd conception of what is simple, Mr. Raven. Let's get one thing perfectly straight. I know nothing at all of Mr. Lamprecht's personal affairs. He's a patient of mine and that's as far as it goes.'

There were blackbirds on this lawn too, devouring the fallen berries with greedy relish.

'He's written a letter,' Raven continued. 'I don't have it with me, but its hardly reassuring.'

The doctor's tow-coloured eyebrows met, bridging his nose. Raven jack-knifed his body erect.

'There's a strong hint of suicide in the letter,' added Raven. 'I understand about professional etiquette but in the circumstances I thought you might be able to help.'

'How?' asked the doctor.

Raven juggled his hands. 'A suggestion, perhaps. I don't know. Some idea of what we might expect.'

Belling was pacing the lawn beneath the tree. His face when he turned was puzzled.

'Mr. Lamprecht has been a patient of mine for ten months. It's no secret that he's a very sick man. I find what you're saying about suicide deeply disturbing.'

Something in his tone gave Raven the clue he was looking for. Barbara's stories of Lamprecht's strange behaviour, his changed personality, the pain-killing pills with the morphine base. What Belling was saying was that Lamprecht was dying anyway. Couldn't it be some kind of brain tumour?

He unwound himself from the deckchair. 'You've said enough, Doctor. Thank you. I should never have come here.'

He called the riverside house from a 'phone box nearby. Zaleski answered. Nobody had called or been there. Raven chose a route that took him near Justice Place. Lamprecht's house appeared to be deserted. The pub by the bridge had closed and the parking space was deserted. He retraced his steps down the lane. Everything was as he had left it, sunlight dappling the ground under the beech trees, the banks, bushes and verges scented and humming with insects. He climbed the fence and went through the kitchen window.

Cigarette smoke had thickened the atmosphere in the unventilated drawing room. The sun had shifted, shining through the dingy french windows to the corner where Barbara Beattie was sitting. The glass-fronted bookcase behind her had been undone and a well-worn copy of *Treasure Island* lay open in her lap. She flicked her hair back nervously.

'What happened, what did he say?'

Her eyes were wide with anxiety as she waited for his reply. It was the kind of look that he remembered from the old days, a dumb appeal for help, the look of a man in the dock as Raven took the witness stand having promised to say what he could in mitigation. He'd never cared too much for responsibility but being relied upon was something apart, and a plea once accepted always invoked a sense of loyalty.

He took the book from her lap and put it back on the shelf. 'I want you to go back to Justice Place and wait there. You can pick up a cab at the bridge or use the Underground.'

She was on her feet in a flash, standing like a great tawny cat.

'What in hell *for*?' she demanded.

Zaleski nodded from the piano. 'Is better . . .' He cleared his throat. 'No air. I am losing voice.'

Raven's glance dismissed him. The only thing that Zaleski needed was a drink. Apart from his short spell in jail it must be the first time in many years that the Pole wasn't making his morning tour of the pubs.

The girl's voice was quietly determined. 'Are you going to tell me what the doctor said or not?'

'Sure,' he said. 'I'll give it to you word for word. He said he was deeply disturbed.'

'*Disturbed?*' He might have been speaking Hindu. 'For God's sake what is all this?'

'You listen, darling,' Zaleski spoke quickly. 'Listen to what he says. I know this man and bloody word of honour . . .'

'Stop being so goddam Polish,' Raven said in a tired voice.

Zaleski lowered his head like a bull about to charge. 'I *am* bloody Polish. I may not be citizen here but I fought for this country. And I say what I like.'

'That's been the trouble ever since you landed.' Raven went back to Barbara and her question. 'All I can tell you is that I'm sure of one thing. Lamprecht's alive and he'll be coming back here. When that happens I want to be able to talk to him man to man. No drama, no emotions. Just talk till he knows that there's nothing to fear. I hope.'

'You hope.' Her freckled nose shortened above a finely-drawn smile. 'Just who in hell do you think you are? Do this, do that. You must be insane. Well, I have news for you. No way am I leaving this house.'

Raven shrugged his shoulders. 'Please yourself, but you stay here alone. Don't bother looking at Casimir. He knows what's good for him, don't you, Casimir?'

Zaleski frowned as if he hadn't fully understood but made no answer.

Her sigh ended on a note of despair. 'It's really something, isn't it? If it hadn't been for you two none of this would have happened.'

'Wrong,' said Raven. 'And that's something else you're going to have to accept.'

She shook her hung head slowly, hair hanging in front of her eyes.

'I'll give it to you straight.' The words evoked another time and woman but he forced himself to go on. 'You're like the rest of them. You ask for help and when you get it you think you've achieved a personal miracle. This has been a very interesting interlude but as far as I'm concerned it can end right here. It's entirely up to you.'

She wiped the sudden tears away with the back of her hand, beaten but still defiant.

'There's one thing you have to know, Mr. Raven. If anything goes wrong, if anything happens to Henryk because of what you're doing, you'll have me to reckon with.'

He made a grimace of resignation. 'You already said that once. It didn't bother me then. It doesn't now. Do you have a car?'

'I have a car.' She recovered quickly. A few seconds with her hand-mirror and her confidence was restored. 'It's parked outside Waverley Court.'

Zaleski winked behind her back, putting his arm around her shoulders. 'Don't worry, darling. I am watching for everything.'

She removed the offending arm as if it were leprous. 'Take your goddam hands off me,' she said coldly. 'O.K.,' she added quietly to Raven. 'We'll do this your way. For the moment at least.'

Raven took them through into the hallway and unfastened the front door.

'Stay put in the house till you hear from me. And whatever you do don't call Dr. Belling. I mean *don't*!'

'Don't worry about me,' she said. Her smile held no warmth. 'I learn very quickly.'

He watched the two figures beyond the bend in the lane and went back to the drawing room. She was the kind of woman who meant what she said. A good lover and a good hater, whereas Cathy had never known what it was to hate. For her, the reverse side of love had been total despair. He peered through the french windows. He could hear the couple next door calling to one another in the garden, discussing the best way to make *sangria*. Apparently they were preparing for some sort of party.

He walked through to the kitchen and opened the window. The yard was out of sight of the lane and he had to have air. He brewed a pot of Lamprecht's coffee and carried the mug into the drawing room. He sat down so that he faced the french windows. A Pole unknown by other Poles in London with a history of imprisonment in Russia. Wife and daughter killed in the Budapest uprising. A man making enough from a translation bureau to support a comfortable standard of living. And finally, a patient described by his doctor as a 'very sick man'. Why had he been disturbed last night to the point of writing what could well be a suicide note? Unless he wrote it before. The truth would be found in the nature of what had disturbed him. Zaleski's drunken accusation of being a Communist surely wasn't enough.

He remembered the look on Lamprecht's face as the Pole came from the cab with Barbara Beattie. The secret lay somewhere behind that brief expression of terror. Zaleski's voice sounded, slurred with vodka and boastful.

'My friend the inspector-detective!'

The words repeated in Raven's mind till he suddenly knew he had the heart of the matter. *Lamprecht was a fugitive*. Raven didn't know from what but the man was hunted and scared. He walked along the corridor to the master bedroom. The shifting sun had angled below the verandah. Specks of dust danced in the broad yellow shaft of light. He looked with new eyes, discarding what he had seen before, and scored immediately. The bed nearer the wall had been shifted recently. The previous indentations still showed in the pile of the carpet. He rolled the bed a few inches away from the wall.

There were blobs of solder on the floor, half-a-dozen scraps of the single-strand copper wire. There was nothing under the other bed. He searched the room again, removing the lining-paper from the drawers, checking the outside of the curtains to see if anything had been pinned there. He was on his knees when faint lines in the ceiling caught his eye. The white-painted ceiling was flat. The lines traced a square that was big enough for a man's head and shoulders to go through.

He wheeled one of the two beds to the centre of the room, jammed it with the other and stuck a chair on the top mattress. He climbed up precariously, keeping his balance by clinging to the wardrobe. The hatch was the same colour as the ceiling and lifted easily off its battens. Dirt fell on his face and hair. He snapped his lighter. The steady flame showed rafters, a water tank and nearer at hand a dirty canvas bag. He dragged it close and jumped to the floor. The bag was stocked with an electrician's work tools, narrow-nosed pliers, files, a range of screwdrivers and some small flat sheets of aluminium. Under these was a rolled-up copy of a magazine fastened with a rubber band. He undid it. There was a portrait of the Virgin and Holy Child on the blue cover, surrounded by armorial shields representing Polish provinces. The lettering was in English.

FEDERATION OF POLAND,
LITHUANIA & UKRAINE
1386–1795
FIRST COUNTRY TO HAVE HABEUS CORPUS
1430
SOVEREIGN PARLIAMENT
1505
FEDERAL CONSTITUTION & PARLIAMENT
1569
ACT OF RELIGIOUS TOLERATION
1573

A felt pen had scrawled the legend *Long Live a Thousand Years of Polish History!*

The mimeographed pages wrapped inside the magazine had been ripped from a pamphlet entitled SMALL EX-PLOSIVE DEVICES. Each page bore the imprint of the Ministry of Defence. He scanned text and diagrams with growing understanding. A man with no life left to live sacrificed nothing in dying. As long as he was armed with the desire, means and opportunity his death could have shattering impact. The Japanese pilots had done it with their suicide bomb-runs. Political assassins had done it, the troubled in mind and spirit, fanatics all with a wrong to right. The question was who or what was Lamprecht's target? He put the things back in the bag and replaced it in the loft.

Two-thirty-five. The coffee in the drawing room was cold but he drank it, sure now of his objective but un-certain how to reach it. He took the 'phone on impulse and dialled New Scotland Yard. The extension answered promptly.

'Detective-Superintendent Soo.'

85

'It's John,' said Raven. 'Congratulations. You've moved up one since last I spoke to you.'

'Intelligence, integrity and perseverance.' The English was perfect, no more than the faintest sing-song betraying the speaker's Chinese origin. 'The hottest day for five years and now you! What can I do for you, John?'

Raven lowered his tone. 'Are you alone?'

'You must be jesting,' said Soo. 'Who is ever alone in this building? But you can talk if that's what you mean.'

'It's important,' urged Raven.

Soo sighed. 'It always is.'

'I need to know about someonce called Henryk Lamprecht, Polish by birth, naturalized British. Anything you can tell me, Jerry.' He spelled the name and gave Lamprecht's Chelsea address. 'Hold it a minute,' he said, hearing a noise from outside. He laid the 'phone on the table and tiptoed along the corridor till he could see through the kitchen into the small brick-paved yard. Someone was rattling the door in the tall wooden fence. A man's voice called.

'Anybody there?'

Raven flattened himself against the wall and inched forward till he could see the driveway. A small pickup truck was parked in front of the house. THOS. MORRISON BLDRS. An extending ladder protruded over the tailgate. The driver stuck his head through the cab window.

'Nobody home, George?'

The second man walked into sight, T-shirted, sweaty and irascible. 'That's the fourth time we've wasted a trip for these bleedin' gutters. Cross 'em off the list.'

The cab door slammed and the pickup drove off. Raven went back to the 'phone.

'You can try C.R.O. but I have a premonition you'll do

better with Special Branch. Have you got any contacts there?'

Soo's voice was tinkling glass. 'What was that you said you had, a *what*?'

'A premonition.'

'That's what I thought you said,' Soo answered quietly. 'My toes just curled. Yes, I've got a contact.'

The truck was coming back up the lane. Raven waited till it had passed.

'Then I'll leave it to you. But keep a low profile. I don't know where this one is going. How soon can you get back to me?'

'Chop-chop,' said Soo.

Raven could almost see his friend in one of his Hong Kong shirts, a wide Buddha smile under cropped blue-black hair. He wiped the stickiness from his throat and neck.

'How long?'

'Half-an-hour, maybe more, maybe less. It depends. You don't want to tell me more?'

Raven hesitated. He'd closed his desk at the Yard with one regret. Jerry Soo and he had known one another since police college days. Misfits by background and character, they'd created a mutual bond that had lasted for eighteen years. Their friendship was firm and needed no affirmation. There'd been times when the little Chinaman had put his prospects on the line for Raven. But this wasn't the moment for explanations.

'It'll have to wait,' said Raven. He gave Soo the number on the dial in front of him.

Time stretched to an hour, an hour and twenty minutes. The sudden shrill of the 'phone echoed through the silent house. Raven grabbed the receiver. It was Soo.

'There's nothing known here but I've spoken with my friend. You could burn your fingers with this one, John. Take care.'

'I intend to,' said Raven. 'In the meantime I'm waiting for an answer.'

Soo's voice was flat. 'He doesn't exist.'

There was no breeze and the air coming into the house seemed to be trapped in the kitchen. A wasp buzzed angrily in the folds of the velvet drapes.

'How do you mean, he doesn't exist?' asked Raven. He wiped the sweat from his face again. 'You just said . . .'

'I know what I just said,' broke in Soo. 'Your man was born in Torun in Poland, real name Henryk Rogala. His father commanded the cavalry school at Grudziądz and was killed at Katyn.'

'So he *does* exist,' Raven said impatiently.

'Not any more,' said Soo. 'He's on the M list. Nobody knows, nobody sees, nobody hears. Only the Dirty Tricks Department. I'm ringing off now, John. There's work to do.'

Raven nodded, looking at the silent 'phone. There *was* work to do. He could start, for instance, by assessing his own position. A friend of a friend, helping out? A charitably-minded bachelor concerned with the plight of the troubled in spirit? A defender of law and order? None of the hats really fitted him. A man's nature didn't change because of a signature scrawled at the bottom of a letter of resignation. The truth was that he was still a cop at heart, responding to the scent of the chase. That and downright curiosity had impelled him. Curiosity, the need to reassure himself of the past, had taken him to Zaleski's restaurant. Then a light touch of guilt, to bring him to the aid of a damsel in distress. Honourable feelings all, by

88

the girl, Zaleski and the ex-Detective-Inspector. The trouble was that justice was administered by mortals and rogues, and the scales were often wrong. The more he learned about Lamprecht the less happy he was for Barbara Beattie. When the time came for tears, someone was going to have to hold her hand.

He'd no idea what he was going to say to Lamprecht if and when the opportunity came. First he had to find him. He could try the third hat and call the local law who would take his statement, thank him and refer the matter to the Special Branch who would pass it on to S Department. In the meantime, Lamprecht could be sitting up on a cloud surrounded by whoever he decided to take with him, innocent or guilty. A direct approach to the Dirty Tricks Department was doomed before it started. He'd heard of the shooting-lodge in a remote pine forest somewhere in Inverness-shire, operatives recruited from the ranks of hard-nosed failures and rejects, an outlaw code of behaviour employed in the final defence of the state, whatever that was supposed to mean. If you managed to find a tentacle there'd be no head. So no Uncle Bill, no Special Branch, no Dirty Tricks Department. There was no one but Honest John Raven.

The fact that Lamprecht was on the M list meant that he was already under surveillance. But the job didn't seem that professional. They didn't appear to know about the riverside house, for instance. His guess was that Lamprecht would be aware of this, that the Pole would be back to put the final wrappings on his package. Under cover of darkness, perhaps. A radio would have been useful. A newsflash might have given a hint. There was a set in the car but he dare not leave Swan Lodge. He lit a cigarette. There were only eight left in the packet. He'd have to ration himself.

He closed the kitchen door and ate a piece of stale cheese he found in the refrigerator. The milk was on the turn but he drank what was left of it. The other two would be doing better. The living room at Justice Place had been full of booze. Zaleski wasn't the sort to let the opportunity go. It was after eight when cars started arriving next door. The lanterns were lit in the trees and the trellis work. Laughter and music echoed back from the river, the sound invading the darkened house in spite of the closed windows. Raven kept close to the 'phone, ready to answer if it rang. Eight-thirty. Jerry Soo would be sprawled on his balcony, a hundred feet above the mud flats and water. His girl would be at his feet, a fringed Chinese doll with a talent and love for music second only to her love for Jerry. Married or not, if they had a child he'd be John Raven Soo. Or whatever name they chose for a girl. Nobody 'phoned and the party next door started swinging.

It was well after nine when he lit his last cigarette but one, standing at the french windows and staring out into the purple velvet. As he looked, something deep in his psyche told him that someone was out there. Eyes and ears sprouted stalks as he scanned the shadows by the river's edge. A vague shape moved near the bushes and then became Lamprecht. The Pole came towards the house, carrying something. Suddenly he stopped, staring towards the french windows. They moved in the same split second, Raven wrenching at the handle of the french window, Lamprecht diving into the cover of the bushes.

Raven burst out, the breeze off the water sweet in his face after the stifling airlessness of the house. His run took him towards the box-hedge, his shout lost in the noise from next door. By the time he found the gap the Pole had made, Lamprecht had vanished among the willow trees. A crack carried in the night as if someone had stepped on a branch and then there was silence. Raven returned to the house, leaving the french windows open. He lifted the 'phone and dialled Justice Place.

'Don't panic and drive carefully but get over here just as soon as you can!'

CHAPTER NINE

Lamprecht, Wednesday

The street was very bright after the artificial light. He stood on the steps for a moment, shielding his eyes, his senses razor-sharp. This interest in his health was no more than a ruse designed to give him a false sense of security. How much they knew or guessed he couldn't tell but instinct told him that he was under surveillance. He took his hand away, his eyes photographing the street. The caretaker from one of the architects' offices was polishing the brass on the door. Further on a man was exercising a poodle. A Ford Transit van without markings was parked, facing Victoria Street. He walked away in the opposite direction, certain that he would be followed. Once around the corner he increased his pace, still looking straight ahead, till he reached Grosvenor Gardens. He waited for the signals to change, fighting off the encroaching dizziness. The spells were becoming increasingly exhausting. The first attack had put a fog between his brain and reality. He remembered the feeling of shocked incredulity as Doctor Belling explained.

It's something you'll have to accept, along with the possible partial failure of memory. Both symptoms are compatible with the tumour's infiltration of the nerve-centres.

He moved forward on the green light, steeling himself to walk in a straight line. The sound of rushing water passed. His ears picked out the click of footsteps somewhere behind him. The small church was on the next corner, a dingy stone edifice with a wooden Christ hanging on a crucifix outside nail-studded doors. He veered left into the cool interior. Lights flickered on the gilt-and-plaster figures of the Holy Family. A small red lamp was burning on the altar. He knelt in a pew, the smell of incense a link with a small boy in a sailor-suit caught in the terror of his first communion. He was alone in the church yet voices seemed to whisper in the shadows beyond the pillars. Then footsteps. He opened his eyes cautiously, his head still bowed.

A woman was sitting across the aisle, hands clasped in front of her, staring at the altar. He looked away quickly, adrenalin boosting his blood-pressure. Failing a hat or veil, a Catholic would have used a handkerchief as token cover. But the woman's short black hair was unadorned. He rose unhurriedly, crossed himself and genuflected and made his way to the confessional-box on the left of the altar. He stood in the dark of the tiny compartment, watching the woman through a chink in the curtain. Her head had moved so that she now faced him. But the lines of pews cut off full vision. All she could see was the top half of the confessional-box. He squatted and took off his shoes, holding the curtain taut as he crept beneath it. He paused for a second, listening. The shadowed body of the church was silent.

He tiptoed away behind the pillar, carrying his shoes

in his hand. The vestry door was closed. He lifted the iron latch cautiously, his body tense as the hinges complained. He could no longer see the woman but there was no sound of movement from her direction. Light filtered through the stained-glass windows. A cigarette was burning in an ashtray on the desk in the vestry. A priest's robe and biretta hung on a hook. Behind the desk was a half-open door, through it the figure of a priest standing in a small flagged courtyard. He turned slowly as Lamprecht emerged, a young man with thick-lensed spectacles. The gate in the railings behind him led to a mews running at right-angles to the front entrance of the church. They faced one another, the priest's eyes hungry for contact.

'You were looking for me?'

Lamprecht brushed by. 'A mistake, Father. I thought of confession but I'm not yet ready.'

The priest followed him to the railings. 'Say a little prayer for me.'

The yearning in his voice followed Lamprecht up the empty stretch of cobblestones. A hundred yards away beyond the corner they would be waiting for him to come out. But it had been too long and he had come too far to fail his wife and daughter now. Vengeance was his not the Lord's. Ten minutes later he was standing in one of the kiosks in the booking hall of Victoria Station. Passengers hurried by, intent on their homeward journeys. Pigeons scavenged the ground near a tea-trolley, indifferent to the listless feet of the Indian who was jockeying it. Nobody looked at Lamprecht. He dialled with his back to the door. A woman's voice answered.

'Two-two-nine, three-six-two-eight.'

Lamprecht wet his lips and spoke in Russian. There

was a moment's silence, then 'One moment, please.'

The next voice was a man's, deep and with a Moscow accent.

'What do you want?'

'An interview,' said Lamprecht.

'The chancellery is closed. Call again tomorrow morning.' The 'phone was dead.

Lamprecht opened the door, letting in the tired breeze from the station yard. A boy and a girl went by, round-shouldered under the weight of their camping equipment. The girl was bronzed and sturdy, her plump buttocks stuffed into cut-off jeans. The same age as Helena. They wandered the world, these children, untouched by evil and full of hope. His daughter would be like that with courage and sensitivity.

He shut the door and redialled the same number. The one he really wanted was that of the Ambassador and ex-directory. The same resonant voice replied. Lamprecht ran the words together quickly.

'I need to see someone in authority, now, tonight.'

'Nobody here,' the voice said. 'Everybody's gone. I already told you.'

'Wait!' warned Lamprecht. He could hear the man's breathing. 'If you hang up now you will be in trouble.'

Caution crept into the other man's voice. 'Where are you speaking from?'

'A public telephone.' Lamprecht read the number from the dial in front of him.

'Replace the receiver and stay where you are.'

Lamprecht obeyed. It was hot in the booth and he was sweating. He held the door open with one foot and leafed through the pages of the battered 'phone-book. An Arab in the next booth was gesturing ferociously with his free hand as he spoke. The 'phone rang, the newcomer's voice quiet but clear.

'Speak!'

'Hurricane,' said Lamprecht. Silence entombed the word for a couple of seconds. 'There is more,' continued Lamprecht. 'I work in Code and Cyphers.'

The response he expected came quickly. 'Where can we meet?'

Lamprecht wiped his neck and forehead. The blue pills were difficult to swallow without a drink but he needed one now.

'There is a wine-bar called Teresa's, a couple of hundred metres up Church Street coming from Kensington High Street. It's on the left next to a shoe shop.'

'I shall be there in half-an-hour. How shall I recognize you?'

'I'm wearing a grey flannel suit.' Dark Tartar eyes rimmed with fatigue stared at him from the oblong mirror. His face had aged overnight. 'No hat, white hair. You will know me. My name is Lamprecht.'

He opened the door. The information would be on its way within minutes to the grey stone building on Dzerzhenski Square. But K.G.B. headquarters would have no record of it. The British had completely buried his identity eighteen years before.

He cut through the main station concourse into Continental arrivals and departures. The boat-train from Dover was unloading. He joined the crowd, waiting his turn for a cab. The gathering lilac dusk increased his confidence. This was life not death. The brief flaring flame that seared the heart and mind free of evil. He'd never see Helena now. There was only Barbie left to understand and it would be hard for her, difficult to comprehend that giving so much could be so poorly rewarded.

He swallowed a pill in the cab and rehearsed his role. Teresa's was a long discreetly-lit room featuring moorish screened alcoves and brassbound sherry-casks. A man with tight curly blond hair in an expensively-cut blue suit was watching the entrance from a bar-stool. He half-rose as Lamprecht neared, ducking his head and greeting him quietly in Russian. They carried their glasses to an empty alcove and sat looking at one another. It was the kind of face that Lamprecht remembered well. Periwinkle eyes in tanned skin, loose full-lipped mouth and ready smile. The face of a Baltic Sea sailor or a prison camp commandant. The bluff hearty manner concealed ruthlessness and cunning. The stranger extended a sunburned hand.

'Sitnikov.' He offered no rank or further identification. He was wearing a white silk shirt and black wing-tipped shoes with buckles.

Lamprecht sipped the nutty wine. The voices from the neighbouring alcove were loud and unconcerned. He could see the trio through the fretted screen, two girls and a man in faded jeans wearing a necklace of shark's teeth. Lamprecht put his glass down carefully.

'I am a deciphering clerk working in the Communications Centre. No doubt you have heard of it.'

Sitnikov found a cigarette case, turning the gesture into assent.

'We broke your code two weeks ago,' said Lamprecht. 'There is a machine.'

Sitnikov lit a cardboard-ended cigarette and exhaled, revealing a bank of gold bridgework.

'There have been many machines.'

'This one works,' said Lamprecht. He lowered his voice even more. 'Hurricane flew into London yesterday.'

Sitnikov's bleached-out eyebrows lifted. 'One question, please. You are Russian or Polish? Your accent . . .' He jiggled his hand. 'It is difficult to determine.'

'Polish,' said Lamprecht. 'That is to say a second-class citizen in this country. On a par with the Negroes and Asians.'

'What do you expect?' queried Sitnikov, a teacher surprised by a pupil's reaction. 'You are the unwelcome guests of an insular and stubborn nation.'

Lamprecht brooded over the rest of his drink then lifted his head very slowly.

'Do you believe in justice?'

The word had a ring in Russian that Sitnikov repeated sardonically. 'Justice? Are we talking about some abstract concept administered by a judge with a boil on his arse?'

'I mean an ethical law,' Lamprecht said obstinately.

The Russian signalled for two more drinks. He thinned his nose, the blood draining away from the bone.

'You Poles are obsessed with the values of language. No wonder you invented semantics. I believe in whatever is suitable for the end in view.'

Lamprecht sipped the second glass of sherry. There was no danger in it. His thoughts had been honed to an edge that could not be turned.

'A way of achieving advantage. Very good. Then we will understand one another.'

Sitnikov scratched at an ankle. The movements he made were brusque and lacking in delicacy.

'Where did you learn your Russian?'

'My mother came from Brest.' The town was almost on the frontier. Wave after wave of Stuka dive-bombers had destroyed the civic centre together with the records of births and deaths.

'So,' said Sitnikov. The wariness in his look belied his genial smile. 'So part of you at least belongs to us.'

Lamprecht showed his teeth like a dog. 'I am for sale.'

The Russian seemed to enjoy the reply. 'You say you have something to offer. But you have already identified the code you have broken. Appropriate action will be taken which seems to leave you empty-handed. Or is there more up your sleeve, good uncle?'

Lamprecht's gaze locked into the bright blue mockery. 'There is the machine itself. A prototype. The research department has been working on this project for over a year. Until such time as you people have it in your hands. the British can crack any code you devise.'

Sitnikov's blunt fingers sought the end of his nose. 'And the price?'

'Hold!' said Lamprecht behind upraised hand. 'I don't know what your function is but your people are well-informed. This device is a prototype and under test. I am the only person trained to operate it. The reports I have made up to now have been negative.'

Sitnikov's expression was guarded. 'What is your official status?'

'First yours,' challenged Lamprecht.

'Major Sitnikov, assistant to the Military Attaché.'

It was probably true since name and position could be checked. A wave of pain slowed Lamprecht's answer.

'I am a senior clerk in the Russian section of the deciphering division with top-security clearance.'

'You have free access to this device? There are no precautions taken to protect it?'

Lamprecht's eyes hooded. 'The building is a fortress with time-locked doors and armed soldiers. There is a direct line to the Alert Room in New Scotland Yard.'

'So?' Sitnikov threw his arms wide, eyes puzzled.

'What was necessary has already been done,' said Lamprecht. 'It is my tour of duty as Security Officer. I am ans-
werable to myself for the safety of this machine. There are
two more days before it can possibly be missed.'

'And then?' The whole of Sitnikov's body was alive
with interest.

Lamprecht shook his head from side to side. 'I am not
so naïve as you appear to imagine. Motive and price I only
discuss with the ambassador.'

'Impossible.' The Russian shifted uncomfortably in his
seat. 'Out of the question.'

Lamprecht lowered his voice. 'Then someone in Department Victor. Whoever is your station officer, your *mokrie
dela* specialist.' He used the K.G.B. slang, 'wet affairs',
the spillers of blood. His wife's murderers had been aptly
named.

'I would have to take advice,' Sitnikov said after a while.

Lamprecht came to his feet. The bait had been taken.
All that remained was to strike.

'The terms are mine not yours. I shall be at Kensington
Palace Gardens at eleven o'clock tomorrow morning.
Which number do I come to, six, ten or eighteen?'

'Eighteen.' The Russian looked up at him. 'With or
without the merchandise?'

'With.' Lamprecht leaked a thin smile. 'You need me to
demonstrate, remember. I shall take my precautions. Re-
mind your friends of it.'

He waited in a doorway. It was rapidly growing dark. An
illuminated bellpush showed a collection of dirty milk
bottles and a card that read:

Jodi, Visiting Masseuse
Your Place or Mine

Sitnikov emerged from the wine bar, scanned the street in both directions like a man with much on his mind and walked to a small black car bearing C.D. plates. He made an illegal U-turn, tyres complaining, and drove off fast towards Kensington High Street.

Lamprecht ate in a room overlooking the river, watching the moths drift through the open windows and die in the flame of the candles. If he kept his head now, there was nothing that could stop him, no defence against an assailant who himself had accepted death. British, Russians, Americans, they all played the same game, filming one another's comings and goings from concealed cameras set up on the street. For all he knew there could be pictures of him entering or leaving the Centre. The beauty of his scheme was its basic truths. The code *had* been broken. A deciphering machine *had* been used. He *was* what he claimed to be.

It was after ten when he left the restaurant. He paid off the cab by the bridge, lit a cigarette and leaned on the parapet for a while looking down. A swirl around the buttress below was the only sign of movement in the black water. His cigarette stub spiralled through the air and sank. There was no moon, no lights along the towpath. He pictured himself in the obscurity at the end, trying to negotiate the railings, slipping on the muddy bank, impaling himself on the spiked frieze. Better approach the house from the front. Dense foliage lined the lane, the trees and bushes absorbing the noise of the traffic. He kept close to the sweet-smelling hedge, his feet quiet on the hardtop. There were no street lamps. He saw the lines of cars as he turned the bend, filling the driveway of the house next to Swan Lodge, jammed up on the grass verge. Music, shouts and laughter billowed from the open windows. His own side-door was bolted. The slats of the fence in the beech trees between the two houses were loose and rotten. He pulled them apart and stepped over the flower-beds onto the grass.

The racket from next door echoed back from the river. Fingers of light pierced the trees as far as the lawn. Swan Lodge sprawled fifty yards away, secret and forgotten and once more a haven. He ran to the boathouse, bent double. Water gurgled in the twilight. There was a sour smell of reeds and mud. Something in the rafters scrabbled through a hole in the roof. He felt beneath the pile of mildewed canvas, relieved as his fingers found the familiar shape of the airline bag.

He was halfway across the lawn, avoiding the brightness shining through the trees when something flared in the drawing room, as if a light had been snapped on and off or a match lit. His heart hammered his ribcage. He crouched low, hugging the bag protectively. He was sure that he hadn't been followed but there was someone in the house. His first instinct was to run but he didn't know where. His mind flew to the letter he'd written, the envelope open, lying on the piano. He crept a little closer, narrowing his brain and eyes on the drawing room windows. The shape of a man's head and shoulders built behind the glass, the tip of his cigarette red in the darkness. There was no need for Lamprecht to look twice. The silhouette was that of Zaleski's friend, the detective-inspector who had been standing in Justice Place. Lamprecht backed off slowly, instinct keeping him facing the danger, back till the shrubbery clawed at his clothing.

The shape vanished from the window and Lamprecht knew he'd been seen. He whipped round and burst through the gap in the box-hedge, holding the airline bag hugged tightly against his chest, on into the alders and willows, the soft earth squelching underfoot. He was moving away from the river, following the line of the railings just discernible in the half-light. The ground was firmer as he came closer to the reservoir. He scrambled up a concrete retaining-wall onto a catwalk and looked back. The house beyond the trees was as quiet as a church.

The catwalk took him past locked pumphouses to the far side of the wind-ruffled water. He climbed a gate and dropped down into a deserted service road. The lighted span of the bridge was directly on his left, movement, traffic. There was nowhere to go except forward. He slowed himself to a walk, carrying the bag as nonchalantly as he could. They were moving in on him, closer and closer. He should have used more finesse, shaken them off without them knowing that it was deliberate.

The pub where he'd lunched was emptying, the car park filled with shouted farewells and the sound of revving motors. A porter was dragging the iron trellis gates across the entrance to the Underground. Lamprecht sprinted for it and the man let him through.

'Just in time, mate. The ticket office is closed. Pay the other end!'

The last train was waiting below, the carriage empty except for Lamprecht. The doors hissed shut and he closed his eyes. It all fitted together, Zaleski's drunken outburst – a man of that type had no control over his thoughts or feelings. The woman in the church. And now this policeman. They'd probably had him under surveillance for days and somehow they'd tracked him home to the river. He opened his eyes as the train rattled into a station but nobody joined him. It could have been worse. The letter he'd written to Barbie was too vague to supply the vital clue they needed. What he had to do now was survive for the next twelve hours, stay off the streets till the time came for the final act, harvest time.

He surfaced at Lancaster Gate, emerging into the welcome bustle of Queensway. It was getting on for midnight but the street was still crowded. Cars were parked in front of packed restaurants. Doorways offered the spicy smell of curry and the sound of Indian music. He found a late-night chemist half-way down and bought a razor and toothbrush. He walked right towards the street running parallel to Queensway. The terraced houses had been converted to small hotels and *pensions*. He climbed the first set of steps. A sign at the top said TRANSIENT GUESTS WELCOME. The plateglass door was locked. He could see a woman in a room at the end of the red strip of carpet. He put his thumb on the night-bell. She turned her head from the television set but stayed in her chair. He rang again. This time she rose and came towards him. She stood, smoothing the wrinkled shape of her dress down over her hips, inspecting him with tired practised eyes. He followed the direction of her gaze, looking down at his stained trousers and shoes. She unlocked the door and spoke without removing the cigarette from her mouth.

'Yes?'

A car drew up behind him. He resisted the urge to turn.

'A room,' he said. 'I'd like a room.'

'Is it just for one night?'

'One night,' he answered. He was inside the door now and standing on the carpet. He could see the car in the mirror, a white M.G. with a couple talking on the pavement. He had to get a hold on himself.

Her veined unstockinged feet were thrust into satin mules. 'Six pounds fifty,' she said challengingly. 'Breakfast included. No female visitors and you pay in advance.'

'I'll take it,' he said and gave her the money.

She led the way up to a room on the second floor and pulled a curtain displaying a hand-basin and a shower-stall. He looked round indifferently.

'I'd like an eight o'clock call if that's possible.'

'Fifty pence,' she answered. 'Everything's possible if you pay for it.' She closed her right eye coquettishly.

'I need nothing else,' he said.

She shrugged. 'It's all the same to me, dear. Breakfast's eight till ten and we like you out before twelve. Good-night.'

She put the key on the inside of the door and he locked it behind her, listening to the slop of her mules on the stairs. There was a New Testament on the bedside table, dead flies in the ashtray. He opened the curtains and lowered a window, letting fresh air into the room. The white car had gone from outside. He swallowed a pill and washed it down with flat lukewarm water. Suddenly he slapped his pockets, remembering. He'd brought two tubes not one from Justice Place. He searched his clothes uselessly. The second tube was either in his locker at the Centre or he'd left it behind at Swan Lodge.

He sat on the side of the bed, staring at the airline bag. His mind filled with echoes. The clear Baltic sky over rye-fields, oxen in a forest clearing, the sweetness of their breath mingling with the scent of pine sawdust, his daughter's laughing face in the back of a haywain. His eyes filled with salt burning tears and he wept uncontrollably. It was his own childhood he was remembering, not Helena's. She was dead as they'd said, murdered with her mother, and death would not reunite them.

He washed his face and sponged his clothes clean. Then he put out the light and composed himself for sleep.

CHAPTER TEN

Slade and McNulty, Wednesday

The black Mercedes was parked in Lawrence Street. The electrically-operated windows had stuck half-way down. McNulty spat through the space with precision.

'I wouldn't mind living like that.' He nodded at the house they'd been watching for the last hour-and-a-half.

It was the last but one beyond the almond tree in the wide flagged walk and built in the style of Queen Anne, redbrick and unpretentiously elegant.

It was hot in the car and Slade eased his back against the plastic upholstery. His gaze found the driver. McNulty's face and hands were burnished as if he lived in some windswept sand dune. His black hair was cropped short, his faded khaki shirt and trousers sharply-pressed. He was a product of the charm school. Orphanage to Army, plucked from the glasshouse at the end of a two-year sentence for removing the lobe of a drill sergeant's ear with his teeth. There were a dozen of them at Priory Park. Anti-social to a man, they did what they were told without question, rebels who'd found both a home and a cause.

Slade fanned the air with his hand. 'Nine to five?

Worrying about paying your rates and taxes? I doubt it, my friend. You wouldn't last a week. You don't have what it takes.'

McNulty stuck the frayed matchstick back in his mouth. 'I don't see no nine to five. This fucker's got it made. Money, a good-looking bird. All right, Slade, you tell me. What makes a geezer like Lamprecht go bent?'

There was one street light near the almond tree. It illuminated the length of the quiet backwater. The blinds were still drawn in the rooms at the front of Lamprecht's house. The shadows of the man and woman inside moved from time to time like giant moths.

Slade jerked his shoulders. 'I try not to think about it.'

McNulty spat again expressively. 'What did they teach you at Eton, Major? I mean what *do* you think when you've got your feet up and nobody's looking?'

Slade hesitated. Queen and Country? A regiment's name dishonoured? 'I think about people like you,' he answered.

'You mean like *us*.' McNulty stitched a smile over small hard teeth.

'O.K., like us,' said Slade.

McNulty flicked his matchstick onto the pavement. 'It's a real pisser, isn't it? I mean you, me and John Wayne. We're all bleedin' heroes.'

The only discipline at the Park was the readiness to obey an order blindly. There was no place for the Nuremberg concept of a soldier's duty to humanity. But McNulty seemed to treat his service as some sort of back-street game for hoodlums.

'Let me tell you something for your own good,' Slade suggested quietly.

'That'll be the day.' McNulty cocked his head.

Slade ignored the interruption. 'You've been spoiled, McNulty. And you're forgetting something. A big head makes an easy target.'

The expression changed on McNulty's face. He shot up a hand in warning and started the motor. The light behind Lamprecht's blinds was extinguished. Both men slid low in their seats as the street door was partially opened. A man's shape showed in the hallway. He stuck his head out cautiously then beckoned to the woman behind him. Both stepped into the lamplight.

The girl was tall with shoulder-length hair, the man almost a foot shorter. They moved nearer the light, still looking right and left.

The girl's hair was auburn, her dress brown, and she was wearing earrings. The man's powerful shoulders bulged in a blue shirt. A scarf was tied in his open neckline. They walked off quickly in the opposite direction. They had been in the house since Slade and McNulty arrived.

Slade opened his door. 'Keep this thing running,' he warned and hurried after the vanishing couple.

Lamprecht's house was in complete darkness. Instinct told Slade it was empty. There had been no sign of the Pole. He trotted past the curtained windows, moving on the balls of his feet. He could see the man and woman from the end of the walk. They were thirty yards away, climbing into a small car facing the river. The street was one-way. He ran back to the Mercedes, wrenched the door open and stabbed his finger at the windshield.

'A green Mini. Something-something L427. You'll get them on the Embankment. *Move!*'

McNulty put his foot down hard, the thrust of the torque snapping Slade's head back. The nearside wheels mounted the pavement, the front bumper narrowly missing the lamp-post.

'Easy!' yelled Slade. The buckle of the seatbelt whipped his fingers as he tried to fasten it.

McNulty grinned and braked at the end of the street. The Mini shot by, travelling west at speed. The girl was driving, the man bolt upright beside her, a monocle fixed in his eye.

'For crissakes!' said Slade. 'We're going to lose them!' The Mini's tail-lamps had disappeared in the traffic.

McNulty winked happily. 'Relax, Major. Relax. You're in the hands of an expert.'

He proved it by gunning the Mercedes in front of an oncoming car. Slade saw it all, the pile of twisted metal hurled against the stone wall, hissing in the river below. He shut his eyes. When he opened them again they were shooting the signals at the end of the bridge. The Mini was twenty yards in front of them, heading in the direction of Putney.

'See what I mean?' asked McNulty, strong-wristed hands firm on the wheel. 'Dare and die, that's it, isn't it, Major?'

Slade looked at him with new dislike. 'You won't last, McNulty. You're not only brash, you're stupid.'

McNulty's face was derisive in the light from the dashboard. But the thought continued to occupy Slade.

The Mini led them through Hammersmith, under the flyover into Twickenham. McNulty drove with cunning, headlamps on, headlamps off, headlamps dimmed. Occasionally he turned from the mainstream of traffic and down some parallel road to pick up their quarry at the next intersection. Acacia trees lined rows of small terraced houses, lath-and-plaster on brick, each with its name on a shingle. There were patches of grass and flowers, forests of television aerials. Slade's sigh was unconscious. There'd be bookcases filled with Reader's Union sets of classics, china animals, ashtrays with fringed leather tassels, people upstairs in twin beds dreaming of escape.

'Where would you say she's heading for?' he asked suddenly.

McNulty's sleeves were rolled up. Tattooed on his left forearm were the words I LOVE NELLY WHOEVER SHE IS. Underneath was a skull-and-crossbones. He nodded at the bridge they were nearing.

'Hampton Court. Maybe Lamprecht's hiding in the Palace.' His laugh was exactly like a goat's bleat.

The Mini crossed the bridge and made a right turn without signals, onto a turn-off beyond a car park. McNulty braked, holding the Mercedes on the crown of the road. The Mini's brakelights showed a hundred yards away. Slade reached across and cut the headlamps.

'Don't lose them but take it easy.'

The narrow lane was sparsely-lit. They followed the trees and bushes to a bend. Glimpses of lighted windows showed beyond cultivated gardens. McNulty slowed just before the curve and killed the motor. He fished a stick of chewing-gum from his pocket and stuffed it in his mouth.

'What is it?' asked Slade.

'They've stopped,' said McNulty. He cocked his head, listening. A car door slammed some distance away.

Slade was out and running. The bend in the lane followed the course of the Thames on his right. He stood on the wheel-scarred verge, watching as the man and woman went through a gate. They vanished suddenly, hidden behind a screen of beech trees. A white-painted sign

109

on the gate bore the name SWAN LODGE. The darkness
and quiet of the sprawling riverside home accentuated the
noise coming from the house next door. Cars blocked the
driveway and lane. He moved closer cautiously, climbing
a fence into the cover of the trees. Chinese lanterns were
strung across the lawn to the edge of the water. People
were dancing to music from hidden speakers, their faces
featureless in the glow from the lanterns. He made his
way back to the lane, lifted the front of the Mini and
removed the distributor head. McNulty had rolled the
Mercedes up on the verge. His voice had the tone and
pitch of a man used to surreptitious conversation.

'The house without the light, right?'

Slade lowered himself through the open door, his buttocks on the seat, his feet on the ground outside.

'They're not at the party, that's for sure.'

McNulty suspended his toneless whistling. 'So?'

Slade unlocked the glove-compartment and extricated
the 'phone inside. He identified himself, waiting till the
call was transferred.

'You can get a room ready,' he said laconically. 'I do
think I've got him. A house on the river near Hampton
Court. There's a couple in there with him, a man and a
woman. No, I don't know who they are, but I shall.'

He put the receiver back in the glove compartment.
McNulty offered his quick mocking grin.

'I like it! Dash and decision, mate. What happens if he
isn't in there?'

Slade took the two revolvers hidden behind the 'phone.
He broke the cylinders on the stubby barrels and inspected
the shells. He gave McNulty one of the guns.

'We start again. And again. And again!' He realized
he was shaking with anger and controlled himself. 'I'm

going to whip you, McNulty,' he added quietly. 'I'm going to knock the shit out of you when this one is over.'

McNulty's tone held the same coiled threat. 'Fair?'

'Dirty,' corrected Slade. 'I want you to have a chance.'

'*Floreat Etona*,' said McNulty.

'*What* did you say?' Slade asked incredulously.

'I can read,' said McNulty loftily. He flexed the muscles in his forearms. 'It's printed in front of that bleedin' book you once lent me. Dr. Heckle and Mr. Jibe.'

Slade hefted the revolver in his hand, suppressing the urge to smile.

'Once we're in that house, you speak when you're spoken to. By me, that is. You answer nobody else and you fire only to protect yourself. Aim at the legs, is that clear?'

'As a maiden's water,' McNulty nodded vigorously. 'Hear nothing, see nothing and say nothing. They taught me that at the orphanage.'

'Poor fellow,' said Slade, tucking the bottoms of his jeans into his Spanish boots. 'There's no justice.'

McNulty narrowed his eyes, lifting his gun at Slade. 'Boom-boom!' he went quickly.

Slade moved involuntarily. The safety catch was off. McNulty clicked it on again.

'Gotcher,' he said with satisfaction.

His histrionics were childish, intended to shock and draw attention to himself. But when the chips were down he was a different man.

A frog croaked in the willows nearby. Another answered. Slade motioned McNulty to his side. 'Look,' he said quietly. 'This is the fourth time I've had you with me. Let's try to do this one by the book. I want to get Lamprecht to the Park as quietly and efficiently as possible, with no involvement of outside agencies. Above all, no civilian police. Is that understood?'

McNulty placed his hand in the region of his heart. 'You can rely on me, Major. I like the fuckers as much as you do.'

Slade hardened his mouth. 'It isn't a question of like or dislike. It's a question of security. And put that gun up the right way.'

McNulty twirled the weapon by the trigger-guard like a movie cowboy. The two men padded onto a half-circle of hardtop. Swan Lodge still looked to be in complete darkness. Slade tiptoed as far as the side gate and found it locked and bolted. He returned to the front of the house. They were singing now next door, in the garden beyond the beeches. He tried one of the windows. The sashes were warped and ill-fitting. He prised back the catch with his penknife. McNulty was close, chewing his gum with monotonous regularity. Slade lifted the lower window and threw his leg over the sill. McNulty came after him. There was enough light from outside to see the strip of worn carpet between the two unmade beds. A child's rattle hung on the dressing table, nursery-posters on the damp-stained walls. Slade put his ear against the door. The sound of a man talking came from somewhere on his right. He turned the handle gently, taking the weight of the wood to stop the hinges creaking. The two men moved quietly towards a crack of light showing beneath a door at the far end of the corridor. This door was shut. Slade stationed himself before it, motioning McNulty to get it open. They burst in behind the swinging door, their guns extensions of their arms.

A candle was burning on top of a grand piano, the man and woman they had followed from Chelsea standing nearby. A second man was in front of the windows leading onto the lawn, a tall thin suntanned individual with longish grey hair, in jeans much like Slade's, a blue shirt and a pair of sneakers.

Slade stabbed his gun in the girl's direction. 'Name?'

Gold hoops gleamed in her ears as she swung her dark red hair. Her fingers flew to her throat and she kept them there. Her voice was barely audible.

'Barbara Beattie.'

The accent was either Canadian or American. 'You!' he said, shifting the gun.

The man next to her adjusted his blazer and inflated his belly. 'Now listen, mate,' he started importantly.

McNulty came off the wall like a panther, grinning as the man went on hurriedly.

'Casimir Zaleski.' The name and accent were Polish but there was no sign of Lamprecht.

'And you?' queried Slade to the second man.

The gaunt suntanned stranger offered upturned palms. 'We don't have twenty pounds between us. You're wasting your time. Why don't you bust in next door?'

It had been a long day and Lamprecht's absence left Slade with a feeling of having made a fool of himself. He lifted his left arm and backhanded the stranger across the mouth.

'*Name!*' he snarled.

The man wiped the trickle of blood from his lips with a linen handkerchief, his voice quiet and well-modulated.

'Raven. John Raven.'

'Empty your pockets!' ordered Slade. He spread out the haul on top of the grand piano. The contents of Zaleski's blazer verified his identity. Raven's eyes were steady above the rim of handkerchief as Slade went

113

through his belongings. Barbara Beattie's brown suede bag held a few pounds and a couple of credit-cards. There were keys and a pass to the British Broadcasting Corporation's Lime Grove studios. He returned the articles to the bag and gave it back to her.

'Nobody moves!' he said to McNulty and went through the rest of the house. It was empty, the beds unmade, some dirty utensils in the kitchen the only sign of occupancy. He noticed that the catch on one of the kitchen windows had been forced. By the time he went back to the others he knew what he had to do. McNulty moved aside in the doorway to let him pass.

Raven was still dabbing at his mouth with the handkerchief. The Pole's belch was sudden and violent. He clapped his hand to his stomach. Slade's nostrils established the smell of alcohol. He had counted on finding Lamprecht in the house. The secret of the man's absence was somewhere in this room. Slade was sure of it. Instinct prompted him to tread warily. The B.B.C. were the last people he wanted to be involved with. He drifted to the mantelpiece with a cautionary glance for McNulty.

'Police!' he said bluntly.

The girl's face showed fear. Zaleski glowered defiantly. Raven seemed to hang like a watchful crane.

'Just what are you people supposed to be doing here?' Slade demanded.

Zaleski and the girl looked at Raven, who answered. 'Shouldn't you show us a warrant-card or something?'

'How about the inside of a cell?' retorted Slade. 'I could show you that with the greatest of pleasure.'

Raven smiled, fingering the small gold lion that hung on a chain around his neck. The smack across the mouth had left him cool-eyed and unflurried.

'Come on, now,' he said ingratiatingly. 'Be reasonable. You charge into somebody's room brandishing pistols and saying you're the police. Surely we have the right to see some sort of identification?'

Slade could feel McNulty's eyes as both assessed the situation. Slade felt in his shirt pocket, producing a small cellophane-windowed holder. The picture inside was regulation size and carried his thumbprint and blood group. He covered the lettering at the bottom and flashed the photograph at each in turn.

'O.K.?'

Raven stuffed the bloodstained handkerchief in his jeans. 'If you'd done that in the first place it would have saved us all a lot of trouble.'

'We'll dispense with the lectures.' Slade waved at McNulty. 'You can put your gun away, Sergeant.' He followed suit, building on what he had seen. 'We had a call twenty minutes ago. This house is supposed to be unoccupied. The kitchen window's been forced and here you are inside. So let's start all over again. Just what are you supposed to be doing here?'

Zaleski was rocking to and fro, his deepset eyes half-closed. The girl seemed to be waiting for Raven to answer for all three of them.

Raven's lighter flared. He leaned his cigarette end into the flame, his shadow long on the wall behind him.

'It's a friend. We just hoped to find him here. He'd taken this place as a sort of retreat. The truth is he's been going through a difficult period.'

Tears were squeezing from the corners of the girl's tightly-closed eyes. Zaleski hurried to her, offering the red cotton scarf from his neck. His face was inflamed.

'So why not behaving like gentlemen instead of primitives?' He wrested a visiting card from an inside pocket and gave it to Slade with a flourish.

Slade read without taking it. 'A Count of the Holy Roman Empire,' he said, looking at McNulty. 'That's almost royalty.'

'My God!' McNulty staggered a couple of paces theatrically.

'I have friends,' glowered Zaleski. 'Important people, not bloody rubbish.'

Slade clapped his hands softly. 'O.K., O.K. Let's wrap this thing up, shall we?' He slapped at his pockets hopefully. Thank God he'd stuck a pen and pad in his jeans that morning. 'It'll be another hour before I get this written up in triplicate and drink my cocoa. I don't suppose you people think about things like that, though, do you?'

'Never,' said Raven.

'Anyone can play,' suggested Slade. Nobody spoke. Three strides took him to the girl's side.

The candle flickered as she pushed her hair back nervously. 'Look,' Slade said persuasively. 'It's almost midnight and I want to get home. What *do* you do at the B.B.C.?'

'I work in research.' Freckles splashed her face and arms and there was a moustache of sweat on her upper lip.

He stared into green eyes flecked with black. 'Then you're certainly not a burglar.' He switched his gaze to the pulse fluttering in her throat.

Her words came in a rush. 'The house isn't empty. I'm engaged to the man who rents it. I was supposed to meet him here.'

'Now we're getting somewhere,' he said with approval.

'*I* forced the window.' The puffiness in Raven's lower lip gave his smile the aspect of a pout. 'But there was no criminal intent.'

'And you?' Slade's finger stopped just short of **Zaleski's** prowlike nose.

The Pole was unflinching. 'When friends are asking for help I am helping. O.K.?'

'I've got a feeling I may have trouble with this one,' said Slade winking at McNulty. They had to be let off the hook but not too obviously.

He spoke to the room in general. 'What time was your host supposed to be here?'

'I don't know. It sounds ridiculous but I just don't know.' The girl's smile broke the last thread of tension between them. 'I'm sorry,' she said softly.

Slade's pen was poised. 'O.K. What's this friend's name? I mean the man who rents the house.'

'Henryk Lamprecht.' She gave it the Continental pronunciation.

'You'll have to spell it,' he said. 'Is that German?'

Her voice and eyes were completely steady. 'British.'

He closed the pad, swinging his look from the girl to Zaleski and settling on Raven's swollen lip.

'You only had yourself to blame, you know.'

Raven's bony shoulders rose and fell. 'The loser generally does.'

Slade pushed his hand out. 'No hard feelings?'

'No hard feelings,' said Raven.

Slade jerked his head. 'When and if your friend does turn up, tell him to get his windows looked at. Goodnight!'

They left through the front door, running as soon as they were out of sight. The car doors slammed simultaneously. Slade turned on maximum headlights.

'Make as much noise as you can going past,' he urged.

The Mercedes roared down the lane, the sound echoing

in the silent trees and gardens. The lights were still out in Swan Lodge but the party next door showed no signs of finishing. Rubber screeched as McNulty drove hard into the curve. Slade felt his jaw muscles tighten and pushed back in his seat.

'Right here!' he ordered.

McNulty swung the heavy car from one side of the lane to the other, slipped it through a pair of open gates and stopped in front of a frame bungalow-style building. Cut-outs of nursery favourites hung in the uncurtained windows. A hand-lettered sign read:

BURGHCLERE PLAY SCHOOL.

McNulty was whistling softly, out-of-tune, and beating time on the rim of the steering wheel.

'Turn that bloody engine off,' said Slade. It was suddenly quiet in the car. The play school faced the river sideways, close enough to hear the frogs' chorus in the reeds. They were a quarter-of-a-mile from the house they had just left. The Chinese lanterns in the neighbouring garden glowed like fireflies in the darkness.

Slade extended his arm, snapping his thumb and forefinger. 'I'll take the gun.'

He returned both weapons to the plastic spongebag behind the 'phone and lifted the receiver. The voice that answered was a known one and trusted.

'I want the following names shoved through the computer,' said Slade. 'Casimir Zaleski, Barbara Armitage Beattie, John Raven. Call me back as soon as you have something and hustle it through.'

He lit one of his long brown cigarettes, wincing as the

match-flame scorched his moustache. McNulty fingered the crease in his pants.

'You don't really think they went for that, do you?'

Slade knew what he meant, all right, but it was too near his own secret fear to be accepted.

'Went for *what*?' he demanded.

'The Old Bill routine,' retorted McNulty. 'Sergeant Bumble and Inspector Fosdick. Even them in there wouldn't have bought it.' He jerked his thumb at the infant-school behind him.

'I'll tell you what they did,' said Slade. 'They behaved like normal law-abiding citizens. It isn't everyone, you know, who's born with one eye on the fire escape.'

'Bollix,' McNulty said comfortably. He stretched his arms wide. 'I wouldn't have minded doing the bird a favour,' he said reminiscently.

Distaste grew in Slade's questioning gaze. He suspected that the girl was a lady. And though it was a long time since he'd had to do with the species he resented McNulty's impertinent wishful thinking.

The younger man spoke as if he could see into Slade's head. 'So where *is* Lamprecht?'

'He'll be there,' Slade said confidently. The words were an act of faith.

McNulty stretched again, yawning this time. 'Suppose he isn't. Suppose them three law-abiding citizens put their skates on.'

'You're full of supposes,' Slade said sarcastically. He whipped the cigarette stub through the window. 'He'll be there because he needs them.'

He added it up still one more time. The B.B.C. was riddled with radical chic and his nose told him Zaleski was phoney. The other man might well be their go-between,

119

the link between Lamprecht's betrayal and its price. The fellow had the right sort of style. He jumped as the 'phone buzzed in his lap. His brain grew number as the matter-of-fact took on a note of facetiousness.

'Here's what you want, Sebastian, hot from the great iron brain. Barbara Beattie negative, nothing known at all. Casimir Zaleski, a stateless national born in Poland. Served with the Fifth Polish Corps tralala. Debts, non-payment of rates, etcetera. He's got a police record of twelve arrests, all to do with drinking. He turned up at the Central Criminal Court a couple of years ago, star witness for the prosecution, a couple of thugs stole a jewelled monstrance. And guess who the police officer in charge of the case was? None other than Detective-Inspector John Raven of the Serious Crimes Squad. This is a real live one – lives on a houseboat in Chelsea and has his own money. He's off the force now but questions about him keep coming up. Special Branch have got a file on him but the details aren't available. The printout's about a yard long. Do you want more or is that enough?'

'That's enough,' Slade said dully. He shook his head, brooding over the lifeless instrument. 'I just can't *believe* what's happening.' He looked up sharply but McNulty's eyes were understanding.

'You can't win 'em all.'

'I don't want 'em all,' said Slade. 'I want this one.' He stabbed his hand towards the lane. 'Back to that fucking house!'

CHAPTER ELEVEN

Raven and Zaleski, Wednesday and Thursday

Raven licked the last trickle of blood from his cut mouth. He'd been hurt and humiliated and resented it. Their ears followed the sound of a car racing down the lane at speed. Raven wrenched at the rusted french-window handles.

'Let's get the hell out of here!'

The girl moved awkwardly, stumbling on the molehills that dotted the lawn. Raven caught her as she nearly fell, looking down at her feet.

'If you can't run properly, take off your bloody shoes!'

They were green kid, elegant affairs that strapped at the ankle. She pulled them off, steadying herself by holding on to his shoulder, eyeing him speculatively. The pair followed him through the gap in the box-hedge and into the crouching willows, away from the noise and music next door. Zaleski wheezed as he ploughed on behind but there was no complaint from Barbara. They were making steady progress into the triangle between the lane and the river. Their line should take them somewhere near the pub's car park. It would have been no good taking Barbara Beattie's Mini. Someone would have been planted there. The breeze off the water carried the sound of traffic crossing the bridge. He slowed suddenly, seeing the railings ahead. Behind them was a concrete escarpment and the wide surface of a reservoir. A faintly luminous light hung above the water. He stood close to the railings making a stirrup with his hands. She stepped from it lightly, leaving the smell of her flesh against his face, poised on the top rail and sprang down, still holding her shoes in her right hand.

121

Zaleski's performance was less graceful and Raven went last, doing it the hard way with arms, knees and elbows. He pointed along the escarpment, his breathing faster than it should have been. There was no flat ridge and they proceeded like children walking with one foot in the gutter. Ten minutes took them to the far side of the reservoir. They negotiated a wooden gate armed with a NO TRES-PASSING sign and found the car park on their right. Raven unlocked the Citroën and wound down the window. He pointed in the direction whence they had come.

'That pair of clowns weren't cops. Not the ordinary kind of cops, anyway.'

The girl was sitting on the back seat, her legs crossed, wiping the soles of her feet. She suspended the action, the brown linen frock hiked high on her thighs, exposing firm rounded flesh and a triangle of checked nylon.

'Just what the hell is that supposed to mean?'

He shook his head at her. 'You might as well make up your mind to it. Your boy friend's in nine kinds of trouble.'

She slipped her feet into the green shoes and fastened the ankle-straps. Only then did she answer and the use of his surname grated.

'You know something, Raven. I'm not so sure that I believe you any more.'

'The worst kind of trouble,' he insisted. Zaleski coughed, beating his chest with the heel of his hand. The pub sign moved in the breeze. 'Do you know what a government agent is?' Raven demanded.

'I've been a senior research assistant for three and a half years,' she said tightly. 'And I still don't believe you.'

'Then you're a fool,' he said. Zaleski was sitting up

very straight, staring at the distant wall as if the discussion had nothing to do with him. A six-wheel truck trundled over the bridge, coloured riding lights high in the darkness, leaving the stink and noise of its passage behind. Instinct told Raven that Lamprecht was out there somewhere, conscious that his world was shrinking by the minute.

'Maybe I'm the fool,' he suggested sarcastically. 'Sticking my neck out for people like you. But it's too late now. I've got to be on your side. I don't like being smacked in the mouth by complete strangers.'

She made a sudden move in the half-light, her fingers brushing his hand.

'I'm sorry,' she said penitently. 'It'll help if I know what's happening to Henryk.'

He measured the words, his voice quiet. 'I'm not sure but I think he's about to do something he'll regret for the rest of his . . .' He hesitated for the space of a second. 'The rest of his life.'

'But *what*?' she demanded.

He shook his head. 'I can only tell you what I think.' And only part of that. The totality was too brutal to explode in her face. 'He's going to try to kill someone. That's what I think,' he repeated.

Her fingers fluttered to her throat. 'I don't believe it. That's impossible. Henryk's a gentle man.'

His breath came and went. He thought of the forty-four-year-old nun somewhere in Quebec. A history of dedication and devotion hadn't prevented her from feeding the rest of the convent arsenic. He clipped the air with his hand.

'The thing is to find him before those other people do. If we keep our cool there's a chance.'

123

Her body was taut. 'But there must be *someone* we can go to!'

He let her down gently. 'There's no one, Barbara. You're just going to have to accept it. There's no one but you, Casimir and me.'

Zaleski turned his hiccup into a belch. 'Ah well.'

'Ah well,' agreed Raven. 'And we could run into trouble.'

Zaleski shrugged his burly shoulders. 'All my life I am running into trouble. It's not my fault.'

Raven turned the ignition key. 'We're going to my place. Whatever comes can start from there. With any sort of luck Lamprecht will be off the streets by now. The real test's going to be in the morning.'

He drove fast, leaving the other two to their thoughts. He left the car in the alleyway opposite the houseboat. Late night traffic trundled along the Embankment heading north and west. He opened the door at the end of the gangway, standing aside as the others went through. Barbara crossed the deck as though used to it. *Albatross* swayed on the wind-ruffled water like some fat-hipped hula-dancer. He opened all the sitting-room windows. Zaleski was pointing out landmarks. Raven dragged some chairs out and pulled the magnum of Krug from the bottom of the refrigerator. The others watched him as he thumbed the cork over the side. Raven filled the three tall glasses and distributed them.

'There must be something to drink to, there always is.'

'*A nos amours?*' Zaleski's glass was already poised.

'Why not?' said Raven. '*A nos amours*. Wherever.'

Barbara put her glass down beside her, pulled a piece of ribbon from her handbag and tied her thick red hair behind her ears. The heat of the day was stored in the night, persisting in spite of the breeze that ruffled the water. Her voice was small but steady.

'I think I'm going to weep. I'd rather do it alone.'

'Straight through, my bedroom.' Raven nodded at the open door.

She rose without a word. Zaleski clicked his tongue. 'Is true what you said?'

The wine was perfectly chilled. Tiny bubbles exploded along the cut surface of his lip.

'I think so, yes,' he answered.

Zaleski helped himself to more wine. Stars were out overhead and the moorings creaked quietly.

'Those men were from Special Branch?'

'Something like it,' said Raven. He emptied his glass.

Zaleski brooded for a minute then grinned. 'Ah well,' he repeated. 'No deportation or things like that because no bloody country is taking me.'

Raven gave him the last of the bottle. 'It won't be like that, Casimir. It's a different sort of world. Whatever happens you won't go to jail. What time does the restaurant close?'

Zaleski looked at his watch, moving his head from side to side. 'Any time. When last guests are gone.'

'Then you'd better get on back there.' Raven came to his feet. 'I'll call you at home first thing in the morning.'

He let Zaleski out, watching the Pole's sturdy figure roll away into the shadows. The Great Dane on the neighbouring boat barked softly in its sleep. It was lying on deck beside its master's hammock. Barbara was standing on the port side, staring out across the river. She turned as he neared and came towards him. She was either unconscious of the appeal of her body or indifferent.

He pulled a chair close to hers. 'You and I have to talk,

young lady. That's why I sent Zaleski home. I'm pretty sure that your boy friend's managed to manufacture some sort of bomb. Not only that. I've got a hunch that we only have till morning to find out what he intends to do with it.'

She bit her lip, close to tears again. 'I just don't understand,' she said desperately. 'He's sick. He doesn't know what he's doing.'

'I think he knows exactly what he's doing,' he said in a level voice. 'And our job's to stop him.'

'A bomb.' She whispered the words as if she only now realized what Raven had said.

He took the watering can to the kitchen again and talked as he sprayed the hydrangea tubs and flower boxes. He asked about her work, hoping she might relax and supply the lead he needed. She watched him from the deckchair, her right arm draped over her head. The sleeveless dress revealed the faintly shadowed armpit. It had been a long time since a woman had slept on the houseboat, and her presence excited him. She could never be for him but what might have been had its own importance. She told him she'd come to England straight from a prairie-province university and had been with the B.B.C. for almost six years. Her mother was dead, her father a veterinarian in Saskatoon. She spoke of her parents with a detached and distant fondness that he recognized. It was similar to the way he felt about his sister.

He had rolled up his jeans and his feet were bare, the water spread between his toes, the warmth and the spray releasing the scent of stocks and carnations. He filled the can again and watered the flowers on the port side.

'I still don't know what you do,' he said over his shoulder.

126

'I already told you.' She pointed at the trough at his feet. 'You've got blackfly in those geraniums.'

He squatted, inspecting the leaves and shaking his head. 'It's earth. A researcher, you said. What exactly does that mean?'

She stretched in the deckchair, moving each limb separately like a tawny cat.

'It means a systematic search for facts and that's exactly what I do. Someone suggests a programme. Politics, history, a social comment. It could be anything and once I'm assigned to track down the facts, nine times out of ten I finish closer to the subject than anyone else on the team.'

He emptied the last pint of water in the can. The Great Dane on the neighbouring boat raised its head and barked like a puppy. Raven peeked through the sitting room windows. The clock on his desk said twenty minutes to one. The stars overhead were as bright as he had seen them in London and a crescent of moon was spiked against the deep violet night.

'Did Lamprecht take an interest in your work?'

'Henryk?' She unbound her hair, letting its red mass run through her fingers. 'Hell, no. The only things that really interested him were chess and music. I mean he accepted everything I did without comment.'

He fetched a fresh package of cigarettes from the sitting room and lit one, leaning against the bulwark.

'He sounds like a very strange man.'

She shrugged a shoulder resignedly. 'It's hard to explain. Have you ever lived with a woman?'

He took a long deep inhalation, releasing the smoke with regret. It curled downstream on the breeze.

'Yes. She used to sleep where you'll be sleeping tonight.'

127

Her face was in shadow so that it was hard to read her expression but her tone was curious.

'Why did she go?'

'She died.' Something made him continue. 'She committed suicide.'

'I'm sorry,' she said in a low voice. 'What I really wanted to say was . . . look, I lived with Henryk to all intents and purposes. Five years during the whole of which he never criticized anything I did. I used to want him to show some spark of feeling. I don't mean about me. I'm talking about my work. Only once was he ever involved and that was last week.'

'Last week?' he cocked his head, the thoughts hurtling through his mind.

She stretched again, her mouth a gleam of white in the shadow. 'We'd done this programme and I'd taken the files back to Justice Place. He had the whole thing out, photographs, articles, even the architect's drawings I borrowed from the Kensington Society.'

He put the question as a man does who asks a direction of a stranger but is confident of getting it.

'What was the programme about?'

'Millionaires' Row. You know, Kensington Palace Gardens. Only three of those enormous mansions are privately owned. The rest are embassies. The idea at first was to point out the lack of security. There's nowhere else in the world where so much damage could be done. Something like twenty embassies in a half-mile stretch that's completely secluded.'

'With the Union of Soviet Socialist Republics occupying numbers eighteen, sixteen and ten if my memory serves aright.' He came off the bulwark as the telephone shrilled in the living room.

It was Zaleski sounding drunk and alarmed. 'They've been here asking bloody questions. Who are you, who am I, who is Barbara. Where we are now, tonight. I don't like it, Raven.'

'Start again,' Raven suggested. '*Who* have been *where?*'

'Those bastards from house on river. They have been here and gone, so watch it!'

Raven glanced through the open windows instinctively but the Embankment offered no sign of danger.

'Go home,' he instructed. 'I'll call you early in the morning.'

The line was silent for a moment. 'Not too early,' Zaleski said finally.

'I'll call you at seven,' said Raven and hung up. He spoke to Barbara from the doorway. 'Would you rather not know what I think?'

She came to her feet. 'I already know.'

'And you'll do what I say?'

'Anything. As long as we're helping Henryk.'

He let her in and shut the door and windows. The guest room was as Cathy had left it. The checked green sheets were hers. Her brush and comb were still on the dressing table.

'There's a new toothbrush in the bathroom,' he said. 'I'll wait until you've finished in there.'

She put her bag on the bed and opened the bathroom door. 'Why are you doing all this?' she demanded. 'What are you going to ask of me?'

'Nothing,' he said truthfully. 'All I want is to leave things tidy. Goodnight and sleep well.'

It was three minutes to seven by the folding clock at his bedside. Relentless light pierced the curtains. It had been like that for weeks now, day breaking in a pale blue sky and bringing the heat of a sun that was untempered until evening. A city was no place to spend the summer. He yawned and stretched, vaguely dissatisfied. There were so many places to see and he could have been in any of them. Bayreuth, for instance, and the Festival. A corn-haired girl with a German accent walked by his side through fountain-cooled gardens.

He reached from the bed and took the 'phone. Zaleski's voice surfaced from sleep, gravel-throated and bewildered.

'Up,' said Raven cheerfully. 'Just get here as soon as you can.'

He went into the bathroom. The shower curtains were wet, the door to the guest room open. She had made the bed, straightened the things on the dressing table. He shaved quickly, ran cold water on his back and dressed in clean jeans and a blue cotton shirt. He'd acquired a blister from somewhere but couldn't bring himself to discard the sneakers. He pulled his lower lip back. The cut was still red. Somehow, he promised himself, somehow and somewhere.

Barbara Beattie was in the kitchen. He opened the secret drawer in the bureau. Twenty-three pounds. He added them to the money in his pocket and took a credit-card as insurance. He joined the girl in the kitchen. She had used the ironing board. Her brown linen frock was immaculate. A bowl of orange and yellow flowers floated in water on the breakfast tray. She must have picked the geraniums through the open window. He poured himself a glass of juice and leaned against the wall smiling.

'Sleep well?'

She looked at him over her shoulder, placing butter and marmalade next to the toast-rack.

130

'Yes, indeed. Do you take coffee or tea?'

'Tea,' he said. The houseboat was moored with her bows facing upstream which put the kitchen on the starboard side. From where he was standing he had a clear view across the Embankment. 'Move away from the windows,' he said suddenly. 'And draw the curtains.'

She did as he instructed immediately, pulling the squares of blue checked gingham across the panes. A chink gave him a line across the wide thoroughfare to the alleyway where his car was usually parked. Something had flashed in the sunshine. A man was standing there, a pair of binoculars trained on *Albatross*.

Raven beckoned her into the sitting room. She followed, bringing the breakfast tray with her. She poured tea and put toast and butter by his side.

'We're being watched,' he said with his mouth full. He lifted the 'phone. Zaleski's number rang without answer. The Pole was already on his way.

She raised her cup, the fingers holding it perfectly steady. 'Will they come on board?'

He made a sign of dissent. 'I doubt it.' Her voice was as steady as her fingers and he gave her full marks. Even the green kid shoes had been polished. 'It'll be the same bunch as last night. Different people maybe but from the same stable.'

He touched the 'phone again tentatively. Jerry Soo didn't leave for the Yard till after nine. He put the receiver down and moved from the sofa to the heavy curtains. The new vantage point allowed him to see the plain van parked fifty yards beyond the mouth of the *cul-de-sac*. They didn't think much of his powers of observation, obviously. It was unlikely that they'd had a chance to bug the boat. The door at the end of the gangway was two-inch-thick oak and impregnable to anything short of a crowbar and only a monkey could have scaled the coils of barbed wire. Come to think of it, water was supposed to interfere with induction devices. He dialled the first three digits of Jerry Soo's number and then gave it best. There were areas into which you didn't take your best friend and this seemed to be one of them.

He opened a window on the port side of the sitting room and lowered himself to the deck. Weeks of sun had softened the caulking. The superstructure was between him and the watcher on shore. The dinghy had drifted during the night and was across the stern on the mudflats. He untied the painter, sat down on deck and braced his feet against the bulwark. The painter started to come in inch by inch and then freely as the rowboat floated. He pulled it amidships, tied up and threw the rope-ladder over the side. It was ten minutes to eight with the tempo of traffic increasing along the Embankment. The line of cars crossing Albert Bridge surged and stopped like a train. The houseboat started to wallow in the wash from the first convoy of heavy-laden barges. He wiped his forehead on the crook of his elbow and crawled along the deck to the stern. The stone parapet at the edge of the footpath was four feet high and gave him ample cover. He sat at the end of the gangplank, his legs dangling over the mud and water, one eye at the keyhole of the mortise lock. It offered a narrow-angled glimpse in both directions. He could just see the top of the stakeout's head, trying to look like some innocent birdwatcher, his binoculars trained on the river. Good luck to him. The heat of the sun would soon strike the alleyway, reflecting from the whitewashed walls.

Zaleski came into sight, looking as if he were joining a yachting party with his rolling gait, blazer and white flannel trousers. All that was missing was the cap. Raven reached up and unfastened the spring-lock. He unlocked the mortise as Zaleski neared, then closed the door behind the Pole.

'Duck,' he said quickly. 'And don't worry about your trousers. We're being watched from the alley across the street.'

They worked their way round to the blind side and Raven leaned through the open window.

'Out you come!'

She swung herself like a gymnast, the movements of her body releasing the scent she was wearing. She had tied her hair with the ribbon and was strangely at ease. Zaleski claimed her hand and kissed it.

'*Cara donna! Belissima!*'

'All right,' said Raven. 'We all know you've got a way with women. Hold the goddam rope-ladder.'

Barbara went down first, shoes in hand, Zaleski next, Raven last of all. He cast off, standing in the bows and pulling the dinghy along the side of the hull to the neighbouring houseboats. A deep bark sounded and footsteps sounded overhead. A green-bearded face appeared, the eyes shortsighted behind grannyglasses.

Raven swayed, raising a hand in salute. 'There's a man hiding in the alleyway. He's bad news, Elliott. If anyone asks any questions, nothing, O.K.?'

The man above made a circle with his thumb and forefinger, his face understanding. His voice was benevolent.

'Cool, man, nothing. And tie all those loose ends, hear now!'

Raven slotted the oars in the rowlocks and pulled on them vigorously. It was weeks since he'd used the dinghy and he caught a crab on the third stroke. Barbara's head was down, her face hidden by a screen of dark-red hair. She was staring at her ankles which were deep in bilgewater. Zaleski was making suggestions from the stern, juggling with his hands to indicate the need for balance. Raven ignored him, paddling the dinghy under the catwalks linking the motley collection of houseboats. People on them were starting the day, cooking breakfast, hanging out washing, shouting and singing. The eight o'clock news was booming from half-a-dozen radios.

The last boat cleared, Raven headed the small craft for the opposite shore. His shoulders lurched forward with the end of each stroke, his gaze meeting Zaleski's wide grin. The Pole appeared to be enjoying himself. He was sitting with the tiller-ropes threaded through his hands, rocking his body to and fro as if coxing a racing-eight. The river was three hundred and fifty yards wide with the current running strong in midstream. A barge sunk deep under paper-waste left the dinghy tossing in churned grey water. Raven's jaw muscles tightened with effort. His back ached and the oars were getting heavier by the minute. It took them a quarter of an hour to approach the south bank. Giant cranes were plucking twenty-ton loads from the jetties in front of the warehouses. He stopped rowing, allowing the dinghy to drift on the current into the cool darkness beneath the bridge. A hundred yards on, he propelled the boat towards the shore, using the oar like a pole. He tied up to one of the Battersea Park landing-stages and held the dinghy steady as the others climbed ashore. The buildings of the Fun Fair showed through the dusty spinney in front of them, the rollercoaster runway and treewalk overhead. The parched yellowing grass was littered with coke cans, sandwich wrappings and plastic containers.

He motioned the others into the shade and unbuttoned his shirt. It had stuck to his back and his palms would surely sprout blisters. The fleet of houseboats across the river had dwindled in size. It was impossible to see beyond the stone parapet to the alleyway on the far side of the Embankment. If the man there had seen their getaway there was nothing he could do about it short of closing the park. The odds were against them involving any form of conventional aid. Everything he'd ever heard or read about them pointed to a policy of preserving their mystique. They played their own rules, cremating bodies in blast-furnaces, burying others a hundred miles out at sea. They were the predators and like all predators preferred to strike unseen.

He lit a cigarette, looking at each of the others in turn. Zaleski's back was against the trunk of a tree. Barbara was putting her shoes on.

'We might as well get this straight,' he said. 'Sooner or later we're all going to have to answer some questions.'

Zaleski fitted a gold-tipped cigarette to his smile and coughed. The girl wiped her upper lip with her handkerchief. But neither spoke.

'The longer it goes the more questions,' added Raven. 'Until these people find Lamprecht or what's left of him. If either of you has something safer to do, now's the time to do it.'

Zaleski blew smoke at the branches above his head. 'So why sounding like bloody Archangel Gabriel? They can ask questions only this time with respect.' He tilted his head like a fighting cock and lifted a monitory finger. 'Ah yes, this time they will learn. I need respect.'

Raven lifted bony shoulders. It was heady stuff, bombastic and yet indomitable. Zaleski believed in himself. Raven spoke to the girl.

'I think Lamprecht intends to go to the Russian Embassy. I think he intends to kill someone there. Maybe more than one.'

Whatever qualms she might have had about Raven were gone or at least suspended. She took a deep breath showing neither fear nor anxiety as if she had reached a turning point in her life.

'If I see him he'll listen to me. I'm sure of it.'

Raven ground his heel on the cigarette-stub. 'I hope so. For our sake if not for his.'

Zaleski had strolled a few yards away, impelled by some rare mood of delicacy. He posed head high, belly hanging over the waistline of his white flannel trousers as though meditating the last cavalry charge.

Raven's fingers touched Barbara's freckled forearm with brief compassion. 'He's dying anyway. He's got nothing to lose. But if he kills anyone in that embassy he's going to blow a hole big enough to bury us all. Think about it.'

She pushed at her tied-back hair with the same nervous gesture, watching him through troubled eyes. 'Dying.'

'You knew?' he challenged.

She moved her head slowly. 'I think I must have always known. Ever since the sickness started. I guess that I never wanted to admit it.'

Raven called Zaleski over and explained. The Pole placed his hand on his heart, ducked his head and then crossed himself. He muttered something in Polish.

The high whine of a hard-hit tennis ball came from a distant court. Raven bent down and retied his sneakers. They were avoiding one another, embarrassed by the threatened presence of death. He straightened up, imposing himself on the silence.

'This isn't going to get us anywhere. The man's sick, scared and desperate. Time is closing in on him and he knows it. I'm betting that today is his day. I've got a hunch that he'll show up at the embassy some time this morning and bluff his way in. That's if he hasn't already established contact.'

Zaleski's slate-coloured eyes sharpened. 'Why establishing contact? If not Communist what is he selling?'

Barbara swung round on him, her face furious. 'Communist? Why don't you lose yourself, you fat phoney? You just won't give up, will you?'

Raven slipped between them quickly. 'He speaks the language. He could have promised anything. All he needs is to get inside that building. We've got to stop him somehow.'

A groundsman picking up paper twenty yards away put his sack down. He glanced from the trees to the dinghy tied to the landing stage.

Barbara shook herself, covering her eyes with her fingers. But there were no tears when she took them away. She even managed a sort of wry smile.

'Not reason but faith,' she quoted. 'O.K. I *know* Kensington Palace Gardens. I researched the title of every house there. It's a private road.'

'But there's a right of way,' urged Raven. In the old days it had been the Diplomatic Protection Group that handled security in the area.

'A right of way,' she agreed. 'But there are police, in and out of uniform. They come and they go. I used to park there but I always had to show my B.B.C. pass.'

He grabbed at the thought and hung on. 'That's it. The

B.B.C. We can't use your car or mine so the first thing to do is find wheels.' He took her arm and walked her to the footpath, motioning Zaleski to follow. The grounds-man watched them out of sight, his curiosity now quite open.

CHAPTER TWELVE

Slade and McNulty, Thursday

The dull rhythmic knocking persisted. It seemed to be travelling up the bedpost and into his head at a point between the eyes. He woke like a cat, lying completely still but aware. He had left the door to the sitting room open. He raised himself on an elbow, looking into the mirror at the foot of the bed. McNulty was lying flat on his back in the sitting room, his tanned muscled body naked except for a skimpy pair of underpants. His eyes were shut tight, his hands locked at the back of his neck, straight extended legs working like pistons. The thudding noise was his heels landing on the carpet.

Slade tilted his head, consulting the waterproof Rolex strapped around the lamp. Seven twenty-two. He swung himself out of bed, kicked the adjoining door shut and locked himself in the bathroom. The flat they were in was a two-bedroom one in a highrise block half-way up Camp-den Hill. The Director himself was supposed to have chosen the location. There were four separate entrances, each one in a different street, with an underground garage and an atmosphere of hushed anonymity that goes with a building that is frequented by wealthy Arabs. Men and women came and went, shrouded in white or pale saffron.

They neither spoke nor were spoken to. The porters in the block minded their own business as if their jobs depended on it.

3A was the corner flat on the ground floor, the lease held in the name of a Mr. Lashti Aram. The rent was paid yearly by banker's draft from Damascus. There were six keys to the steel-lined front door and its impregnability was guaranteed by Chubb & Sons Lock and Safe Company. The telephone number was ex-directory and the flat was linked to Priory Park by a specially installed private line. The only people who slept there or visited were field agents on a Metropolitan assignment.

Slade spat a mixture of water and toothpaste into the bowl and rinsed his mouth. The two electric razors were filthy as usual and neither had a moustache trimmer. A unit came up from the Park twice a month, allegedly to clean out the flat. But as far as he could make out, they spent their time drinking beer and playing cards. He combed his hair carefully, prolonging the time until he faced McNulty. They had called off the hunt at two in the morning with Raven and the girl on the houseboat and showing no signs of leaving.

Slade had reported back to the Park and the Duty-Director's remarks still sounded in his brain.

I hope you're right, Sebastian. Just don't lose him. This joker's red hot.

The trouble was that they *had* lost him. Lamprecht had gone up in smoke like some stage demon. Slade dropped the dirty towel in the linen-basket and went into the bed-room. He raised the blind, flooding the dusty carpet with sunshine. The top of the dressing table was ringed with the souvenirs of dirty glasses. Someone should complain but nobody did. The flat had been furnished from a

Harrods catalogue, the colours and fabrics meant to be the choice of a Damascus merchant. He opened the door to the sitting room. McNulty was sprawling on the sofa, neat-haired and frowning over a newspaper. There was a plate of biscuits, a teapot and two cups on the table at his elbow. One of the cups was filled with a pale brown brew. McNulty lifted his burnished face.

'The biscuits are stale and there's only one teabag. No milk.'

Slade filled the spare cup and took it to a hideous chair upholstered in patterned green velvet. There was an oil-filled glass case on a stand, its ripple of colours set in motion by the sunlight.

'Do you always snore like a pig when you sleep?' Slade demanded.

'That's what they say.' McNulty showed strong white teeth.

Slade tasted the tea and grimaced. 'Christ!' he said feelingly. His gaze fell on the paper on McNulty's stomach. 'Is that today's newspaper?'

'Nothing much in it.' A look of resignation invaded McNulty's face as if he knew what came next.

'Where did you get it?' Slade's voice was patient.

McNulty threw an arm at the front door. 'Nicked it. Up on the next floor. It was too early to score any milk.'

Slade set his cup down carefully. His Spanish boots were dirty, his silk shirt creased, yet McNulty's khaki pants were immaculate. He must have slept with them under the mattress.

'I could black you for that,' Slade said quietly.

McNulty rolled on his side. 'Not you, mate. You've got too much style.'

A telephone rang but the call was in the next flat.

McNulty had replaced the keys where Slade had left them. Slade looked at his watch. It was ten past eight. The car was in the basement garage.

'We'd better make a move. We can grab something to eat on our way there.'

McNulty was already on his feet. Slade heard the crash as the tea cups were tipped into the sink. McNulty emerged from the kitchen, popping a stick of gum in his mouth.

'On the way *where*?'

The question seemed innocent but Slade fumbled the answer. His irritation grew every time he thought of Thoroughgood. Old farts like that should be left at their university desks.

'We're concentrating on the girl and this Raven. Either Lamprecht comes to them or they go to him. Those are our options.'

McNulty straightened the cushions where he had been lying, giving one last admiring pat to his handiwork.

'I thought we were going to turn that house over again in daylight.'

'We are.' Slade collected the flat-keys from the table. 'Do you mind if we do this my way, McNulty?'

'Absolutely not,' McNulty said cheerfully. He jigged a couple of steps to the music coming from next door, his arms moving in rhythm. 'I've three days coming to me when this one's over. Them birds are going to love it.'

'*When* this one's over,' Slade repeated meaningly. The younger man's cover as a chauffeur in a government pool was phased to account for his absences.

McNulty spoke as Slade was about to open the front door. 'What does Irregular War Service mean?'

Slade released his grip on the door-handle and turned around slowly.

'Just what are you talking about?'

McNulty bounded closer on the balls of his feet. 'It's written on your file in Records.'

Slade's mouth was suddenly dry. A polished corridor stretched in his mind, the windowless room at its end protected by the Park's electronic security system.

'And when were you in Records?'

McNulty grinned happily. 'It's a long story, Major. All that bleeding basic training, remember. If you teach a dog to bite you better watch your arse. I can go through the Centre like the Invisible Man. You know, it helps when you salute for your breakfast like we do.'

Slade shrugged in disbelief. 'You're not right in the head, McNulty. I'm going to have to put this on paper. You realize that?'

McNulty's grin widened. 'Don't get your bowels in an uproar. Them records are nothing but holes in cards. There's only three things in writing on yours. Your name, your age and what I said. Irregular War Service. I thought you'd like to know.'

'You're crazy,' said Slade. 'And a head case. I'm dead serious, McNulty. I'm going to have to write you up.'

It was like warning a freefall parachutist half-way down that his ripcord has failed. McNulty's grin was unabashed.

'Some you win and some you lose; the truth is I don't really *give* a fuck, Major.'

Slade looked at him long enough to realize that he meant what he said and opened the door.

'Let's get out of here,' he said quietly.

The walls of the basement garage were tiled. A mechanized turntable at the foot of the two ramps distributed the cars to the two underground floors. A checker wearing what looked like a white spacesuit spoke into a microphone. Seconds later the Mercedes rolled out of the elevator. The paintwork had been washed and polished to a high gleam, the interior vacuum-cleaned. The two guns and the radiophone were in the locked glove compartment. The key was on Slade's ring.

McNulty took the wheel, suspending his gum-chewing whistle at the shining front.

'It's about the only time this thing ever gets cleaned. Where to, Major?'

'Stop at the bottom of Campden Hill,' ordered Slade.

McNulty's eyes were strangely bright and he was very sure of himself, almost complacent. Slade had never seen McNulty drunk though rumour placed the younger man high in the league of hard-drinking roisterers.

They coasted up the ramp and turned left. McNulty braked just before coming to Kensington High Street and angled the big black car to the kerb. It was twenty to nine with barelegged girls in flimsy frocks and men in shirt-sleeves hurrying on their way to work. The sun was still low but awnings were already being cranked down in front of shop windows. Slade called the observation van on the radiophone.

Sanglier answered, a French-Canadian from the R.C.M.P. on an exchange course. His accented voice was laconic.

'Allo, oui, bonjour! Ees nothing much to report. The Polish arrive ten minutes before. They are now three on the boat.'

Slade glanced at his watch. Eight fifty-two. 'Where are you parked?'

'Where I was told.' Sanglier's temper was notoriously fragile. 'By the river, maybe three hundred metres from the boat, perhaps.'

'And Trent?'

'I cannot see round corners but I think he is still in the alleyway.'

'Move the van,' ordered Slade. 'Get yourself onto one of those side streets. This character knows as much about this game as we do. And tell Trent to circulate. He'll take root if he stays in the alleyway. Call me back the moment anyone boards or leaves the houseboat.' He replaced the 'phone and looked at the other man. 'O.K.,' he said softly. 'What's the joke?'

McNulty shifted his gum across his grin. 'I was just thinking. If the other fellow's smart he could be a thousand miles away by now.'

'If your aunt had balls she'd be your uncle,' Slade said sourly. They had established the numbers of Lamprecht and Raven's passports before midnight, the girl's an hour later. There was no record of a passport being issued to Zaleski but his description had been added to the Stop and Detain notice operating at all ports of exit. There would have been news by now if Lamprecht had been sighted.

He used the 'phone again, this time to call the Park. 'Slade. It looks good from here. Three of them on the houseboat. Either they go to Lamprecht or he comes to them.'

The Duty-Director's voice was dispassionate. 'I hope you're right because I'm getting a lot of flak from Thoroughgood. He's been on the line twice since eight o'clock, asking for you in the first place and then giving me the benefit of his oratory.'

Resentment bubbled in Slade's brain. 'What the hell does this old woman want from us! He's the one who called us in.'

'Not Thoroughgood. Somebody else. Thoroughgood's

the Great White Father and Lamprecht's one of his good Indians. All I'm saying is be successful. I'm sure you can and will.'

Slade dropped the flap of the glove compartment. 'Drive to West London Air Terminal.'

The concourse was crowded with buses bound for Heathrow. Taxis scurried through like beetles. Slade pointed at a slot stencilled OFFICIAL PARKING ONLY.

'Stick it in there,' he instructed. They took the lift up to the main hall and took seats in the cafeteria section. People were milling around the booking and check-in counters, changing money, buying books and dozing on benches. The announcements of flight departures flickered on television screens, reinforced by messages over the public-address system.

Slade ordered breakfast. Something was niggling at the back of his mind, struggling for recognition. It was something McNulty had said.

He attempted to eat the bacon and eggs then pushed the plate aside. The glass of water he'd asked for was luke-warm and tasted of chloride.

'The pigs were fed on salt and the hens ate straw,' he said.

McNulty reached across and took Slade's plate. 'You've been spoiled, Major. Wait till you try the grub in the glass-house.'

Slade felt in his shirt pocket for a sliver of ivory mounted on silver. He used it to extract some bacon shreds from his teeth. 'I've never been to prison, McNulty, not even a military prison and I've no intention of going.'

McNulty demolished the food in one forkful. He wiped the plate with a limp piece of toast and closed an eye.

'Say you don't know. It can happen to anyone.'

Slade lit a cigarette. 'You're sure you're finished? There's nothing else you fancy, a dish of sausages or something?'

McNulty shook his head, rapping himself on the breast-bone. The resultant belch turned the head of an Asian collecting crockery nearby.

'No, that was delicious, Major. Couldn't have been better.'

Slade's grin was involuntary. McNulty was a natural rebel who chose his own disciplines. He was untouchable. It was this that fascinated Slade. He paid the bill and looked at his watch again. It was getting on for nine-thirty. He glanced across the table.

'Did you mean what you said in the flat? About not caring whether you stayed in the service?' He asked the question on impulse.

McNulty's eyes were cold behind his smile as he found a fresh stick of gum.

'I'm a survivor like you, Major. You and me do what we do for money, right?'

A quartet of Hong Kong Chinese moved into the next booth, square-smiling and delicately-boned. Slade pitched his voice below their nasal patter.

'As it happens you're only partly right. There are other considerations.'

'O.K., give me a frinstance,' challenged McNulty.

It was difficult to explain the fear of failure, the fear of one's weaker self.

'It isn't easy,' said Slade. 'I mean to explain.'

'It is for me,' said McNulty. 'I never had none of the things you had and I don't bleedin' well want them. As long as they pay me and keep off my back I'll do the job.'

Slade nodded understanding. His earlier threats seemed ridiculous. McNulty's courage was unhampered by imagination, his readiness to destroy proven on three occasions. The Disciplinary Board wasn't about to take his invasion of the Records Office any too seriously. Slade came to his feet.

Outside a ticket was stuck under one of the Mercedes' windscreen-wipers.

THIS SPACE IS RESTRICTED TO THE USE OF OFFICIAL PERSONNEL. A REPETITION OF THIS OFFENCE MAY RESULT IN A PROSE-CUTION.

Slade tore the ticket in two and deposited it in the nearest litter-bin.

'Let's take a look at Justice Place.'

It lay quiet and secure in the sunshine. They parked by the lamp post at the end. A child was crying in a pram beneath the almond tree but the cry was half-hearted, the woman at the open window opposite undisturbed. A life-time ago he had lived in just such a house, Regency-striped walls, bright anonymous furniture, insurance policies with a string of pearls in the wall safe and dread-ful Margaret. Margaret for breakfast, Margaret for walks and Margaret for bed. Nothing eventful ever happened and he had been drowning in a sea of platitudes. Divorce had been hard won, Margaret fighting with a ferocity he had only suspected, landing him with legal costs that had followed him into the Army.

He pointed at Lamprecht's house. The bottle of milk on the doorstep was curdled.

'As dead as a dodo.'

A man emerged from the house next door as he spoke. He was dressed in a striped blue flannel suit, a white hat with a large brim, and carried a briefcase. He came towards them quickly with the high-kneed action of a hackney, the young keen executive, glancing sharply sideways as he passed the Mercedes.

'I want to bet he'll be back,' said McNulty nodding at the retreating figure. 'This is a high-class manor and you and me don't look kosher.'

He grinned as the man turned abruptly and went to McNulty's window. His voice was polite but firm.

'Are you looking for someone? Can I help you?'

McNulty sank lower in his seat, jerking his thumb at Slade. 'Ask him, mate. I'm only the driver.'

'We were looking for Mr. Lamprecht,' Slade put in quickly. 'Number six.'

There was egg on the man's lower lip and his eyes were bloodshot. 'Then I'm afraid you're out of luck. He's away.'

McNulty was whistling softly between his teeth. 'You don't know when he'll be back?' queried Slade.

'I don't,' said the stranger. He seemed to be considering whether or not to give them the benefit of the doubt. 'We haven't seen him for a couple of days. But his girl friend was here yesterday. I do know that because my wife spoke to her.'

'Ah well,' said Slade. 'Thanks all the same.'

The man made a tentative gesture. Slade could see him in the rearview mirror, watching the Mercedes as it drove away. A couple of hundred yards further on the buzzer sounded in the glove compartment. He took the radio-phone. It was Sanglier from the van.

'A woman has just arrived to the houseboat.'

'Where are you?' asked Slade.

'Old Church Street. In face of the river.'

'We'll be with you in five minutes.'

148

McNulty drifted the heavy car into a turn. 'Correct me if I'm wrong but I've got a feeling we're not doing too well.'

Slade glanced at him sharply but McNulty's face was innocent. 'We're not,' answered Slade. He stopped the Mercedes a hundred yards from the van. 'Move this thing around the corner and wait for me there.'

Traffic flashed by at the end of the street, hurtling along the Embankment in both directions. He hurried down to the van and climbed into the cab beside Sanglier. The squat French-Canadian was wearing shorts, sandals and a creased black T-shirt. A tiger's claw was suspended on a piece of string around his neck. The puckered scar deforming his jawline was a souvenir of a knife fight. Slade angled his body so that he could see most of the houseboat through the dirty windscreen.

'O.K., let's have it,' he said shortly.

Sanglier scratched delicately through the black forest of hair on his forearm.

'She goes in with a bag and a key. A little woman, maybe sixty years old. She look like a cleaner.'

Slade could just make out the door at the end of the gangplank, the coils of barbed wire stretched on top and at each side.

'What about the other three?'

Sanglier's shoulders lifted expressively. 'No one has come from the boat.'

'And Trent?'

'Ask heem.' Sanglier pointed at the walkie-talkie on the seat between them. 'He is not liking what you said about taking root.'

Trent reported his position from the Albert Bridge three hundred yards away.

'Stay where you are,' ordered Slade. He worked his way round behind the buildings facing the houseboats, across the Embankment and onto the bridge. Trent's fat form was at the top of the rise. He was leaning over the parapet, staring down at the water that swirled round the piers below. Slade wasted no time, pushing his hand out.

'Give me the glasses.'

Powerful lenses dragged the image close. He shifted the glasses, scanning the tangle of wires and washing, the gaily-painted superstructures and television aerials. *Albatross* was moored apart from the others, her sturdy hull buttressed by truck tyres. All the windows and doors in the living quarters were wide open. A woman was hanging some towels on a line strung across the foredeck. He lowered his field of view fractionally, his attention caught by a dangling rope-ladder. He revolved on the heel of his boot, his eyes behind the binoculars finishing on a landing stage on the south bank of the river. The dinghy tied there bore the word *Albatross* painted on its stern. He returned the binoculars. It was a while before he trusted himself to speak.

'You know what you've done, I suppose?'

The fat man was hatless and sweaty. He turned his red face towards the distant dinghy.

'I only just got here,' he said defensively.

Slade's voice cracked. 'You let them row away under your nose.'

The fat man was struggling with the field glasses and walkie-talkie set, his movements and body cumbersome.

'I can't cover two sides at once, you know.'

'What did you expect?' challenged Slade. 'A twenty-gun salute to tell you they were running? Fuck off and keep that gangway under observation.'

A passing truck drowned the fat man's retort but his face turned a deeper shade of red.

'Nobody tells me to fuck off.'

'I just did,' Slade said dangerously. 'I didn't mean in that way, but I can if you want me to.'

He walked from the bridge, feeling the fat man's glare planted between his shoulder blades. He was half-way back to the Mercedes when he suddenly remembered what it was that was bothering him.

McNulty had the car door open and waiting.

'Trouble?'

Slade shut his eyes momentarily. When he opened them again the motor was running.

'We lost them,' he said bitterly. 'That clown let them row across the river and thumb their noses at us.'

McNulty clucked with his tongue. 'So now what?'

'Back to Hampton Court,' said Slade.

The narrow lane under its leafy canopy twisted before them, as peaceful as a forest track. The green Mini was still up on the grassy verge, jammed against the screen of rhododendron bushes. The rotor-arm was on the ledge in front of Slade. He signalled McNulty to turn the Mercedes into the Swan Lodge driveway. The bedroom window was as they had left it the night before, half-an-inch of daylight showing between the sash and frame. The sight of the house reminded him of Raven. It was the second time in twelve hours that the man had made a fool of him and the thought rankled.

'I'd like to put a hole in that beanpole's brainpan,' he said bitterly. 'I'm talking about that ex-cop. He's in this up to his ears.'

McNulty switched off the motor, yawned and threw his

arms wide. 'I'm getting bad vibes all round. None of it makes any bleedin' sense to me.'

Slade looked at him absently. The party in the house next door must have continued late. Broken glass on the lawn winked in the bright sunshine. Chairs lay overturned and one of the lanterns was still burning under a beech tree. The house itself was firmly closed against all sorts of interruption.

'Bad vibes,' McNulty repeated, shaking his cropped black head. 'I think I'd sooner be up in Scotland, Major, wouldn't you? There's nothing like a straight touch of the old mayhem, especially when you can't get nicked for it.'

Slade's head turned slowly. He'd achieved something over the past few years, the ability to close his mind on things best forgotten. And he was glad of it.

'You've got a vivid memory, McNulty. Take care that it doesn't land you in the shit.'

McNulty's eyes were as untroubled as a Highland loch. 'What's the use? I'm always in it in any case.'

The two men looked at one another as the sound of an engine invaded the peace of the lane.

'Police,' Slade said quickly. 'Let me do the talking.'

The Panda car stopped as it came abreast of the abandoned Mini. The uniformed driver checked the licence numbers against a list in front of him. He pushed back his cap and drove on. Slade was out of the car and forcing the window up. McNulty followed him over the sill, swearing as the sashcord broke, the windowframe falling on his back. The two men stood out of sight as the police car returned. Then the lane was quiet again. Slade came off the wall.

'O.K., this is your idea. What are we looking for?'

McNulty's pivot took in the narrow unmade beds, the

ratty strip of carpet between them, the fly-spotted nursery rhyme posters.

'Some kind of a magic hat, I suppose. You stick it on your bleedin' head and bingo you're invisible.'

An avalanche of unsolicited mail covered the floor behind the front door. The sparse furniture was shabby in daylight, paper peeling on the damp-stained corridor walls. He walked as far as the drawing room. The french windows were open.

He stared towards the river at the end of the lawn, imagining Raven's thoughts as he tiptoed with the others away in the darkness. While *he'd* been sitting in the car trying to make up his mind what to do with them. He called along the corridor to McNulty. The sap had gone from his hope. They were wasting their time in this place.

'Take the big bedroom!'

He moved forward into dusty sunshine and lifted the top of the grand piano. He let it fall with a jangle of wires. They were as likely to find a magic hat here as anything else that would help them. He swung quickly as a shout echoed through the house. McNulty was standing in the middle of the chintz-curtained room, pointing at the ceiling.

'The cracks! See them cracks? There's a loft up there.'

They dragged a couple of chairs from the wall and stood one upon the other. McNulty climbed up, Slade holding him by the ankles. The hatch lifted in the ceiling, dislodging dirt that showered their heads and faces. McNulty reached into the darkness and dropped a small canvas bag at Slade's feet. A rolled-up magazine followed. McNulty landed like a cat, relaxed and watchful. He wiped the cobwebs from his drill shirt, grimacing.

'Someone's been up there not too long ago. There's marks in the dust.'

The canvas bag held a complete range of electrician's implements together with a soldering iron and sheets of aluminium, a roll of plastic-covered flex. Slade peeled the rubber band from the tightly-rolled paper. There was a magazine decorated with the armorial shields of Polish provinces emblazoned on the cover. Someone had scrawled a patriotic slogan across the glossy paper. The mimeographed sheets inside dropped to the floor. Slade picked them up. They had been ripped from a handbook and the text was in English. He wiped the back of his neck, looking down at the page-headings.

SMALL EXPLOSIVE DEVICES

A loud singing sounded in his ears and his voice sounded remote. 'Jesus *Christ*!'

McNulty moved his head quickly. 'I told you, bad vibes.'

Slade kicked the chair out of the way and started pulling drawers open. All he could find were some snippets of wire on the carpet. McNulty was squatting on his haunches, reading through the papers Slade had let fall. His burnished face was expressionless.

Slade slammed the wardrobe door with a deep feeling of certainty. He turned and spoke slowly.

'We've been barking up the wrong bloody tree. Lamprecht's no traitor.'

McNulty rose, wiping his hands on his hips. He passed the papers to Slade, eyes narrowed in anticipation.

'Then what?'

Slade's laugh held no joy. 'We've been wrong from the

start, the whole bloody lot of us. What we've got here is a bunch of fucking lunatics.'

McNulty stuck out a warning finger. 'Don't give me no riddles, mate. Not at this hour of a morning!'

'He's a bomber!' Slade fired the words with conviction. He jammed the papers in his hip-pocket and picked up the canvas bag.

'I don't like it.' McNulty wagged his head. 'I don't like the sound of it.'

The pieces were clicking into place in Slade's mind. Not one of them was seemingly related yet the composite picture was perfect. He glanced at his watch. Ten thirty-five.

'Let's get out of here.' They left by the front door. McNulty's expression had sobered considerably, his face honed as fine as a deerbone.

Slade checked the guns in the glove compartment and put them back behind the radiophone. There could be no contact with the Metropolitan Police, not even with the Park, not until he'd played his cards. He put the question quietly, smiling to take off the edge.

'You want glory, don't you, McNulty?'

McNulty started the motor, glancing suspiciously sideways. 'How do you mean, do I want glory?'

Slade jerked his head at the lane. 'Glory and the acclaim of your superior officers. Move it, McNulty, we're making history.'

Gravel spattered the windows behind as McNulty reversed the Mercedes. 'Is it all right if I know where we're going?'

Slade's voice was level. 'Notting Hill Gate. Kensington Palace Gardens.'

CHAPTER THIRTEEN

Lamprecht, Thursday

He woke suddenly, his brain a split second ahead of the telephone bell. The voice sounded through a chatter of pidgin English.

'Eight o'clock, mister.'

The watch on the bedside table was a couple of minutes late. 'May I have some breakfast?' At the back of his mind was the thought that everything must appear to be normal.

'Cooked or Continental?'

'Just toast,' said Lamprecht. 'Toast and coffee.'

He put the 'phone down. There was a copy of the New Testament beside it. Someone had scrawled across the fly-leaf.

> *Who lives more lives than one*
> *More deaths than one must die.*

The room was airless and oppressive, sealed by the heavy curtains. He opened them and lowered the window still further. The boxes of geraniums below had been watered, the masses of pink and red flowers gently steaming in the sunshine. The park was no more than a couple of hundred yards away. Dust rose beyond the railings as a group from a riding school cantered by. It would have been good to walk there this one last time, to feel the grass beneath the great oak trees. But there was no chance. He could not risk an appearance on the streets. They'd be looking for him everywhere by now. When he left the hotel the move must be final. He showered and shaved, using the unfamiliar razor awkwardly. He dressed in the grey flannel suit, resenting the fact that his clean shirt and underclothes had been left at Swan Lodge. The truth was that a simple visit to a restaurant had brought all his careful planning to the brink of failure. He unlocked the door in response to a gentle knocking. A smiling Sinhalese girl with glossy braided hair carried in a breakfast tray. He relocked the door behind her and took the tray to the window. Two small girls in school uniform were hurrying along the street hand-in-hand. He looked away deliberately, blocking his ears to the sound of their voices. He ate slowly, without taste or interest, forcing himself to swallow. He was attempting to cover his apprehension with familiar routines.

He bolted a couple of pills, washing them down with the gritty coffee. A pair of crows flopped from a chimney opposite. He watched their flight towards the park, sage cunning birds, mixing with no other species, making no concessions to an urban existence yet somehow managing to survive.

It was twenty minutes past nine when someone knocked on the door again. He spoke through the crack.

'What do you want?'

'Can I do your room now, sir?'

'Later,' he said. 'I do not want to be disturbed. I am here until half-past ten.'

A carpet sweeper droned on the staircase outside. He seated himself at the window and leafed through the New Testament. His mind refused the message of hope. If what the priests had taught him was true a single act of contrition could atone for the foulest crimes, even those of a butcher like Butov. He threw the book on the bed. No. Judgement and sentence were contained in the canvas bag by the table. Beyond that was oblivion, for himself as well as for Butov. There was neither justice eternal nor injustice but at least his life would not have been lost in vain.

It was ten o'clock, time to make the final inspection. He lifted the machine from the airline bag. His work had been patient and thorough, reproducing an outward facsimile of the codebreakers at the Centre. Only the interior was different. He removed the retaining screw in the base with a coin. The aluminium plate concealing the charge of plastic and detonator fitted flush. The switch that would activate the explosive was hidden under the Cyrillic keyboard. The detonation would be instantaneous. He screwed the base back on, zipped the machine in the bag and used the 'phone. He gave the woman the number he had dialled before. The embassy switchboard answered.

'I wish to speak to Major Sitnikov,' he said in Russian.

A series of clicks linked him with an extension. 'Sitnikov.'

Lamprecht's voice was steady. 'I will be there in three-quarters of an hour. With the merchandise.'

'Good. And remember, number sixteen.'

The danger signals flared again in Lamprecht's head. He had studied the architectural drawings and photographs from the B.B.C. library till he felt that he knew every inch of the three Soviet buildings.

'Why not the embassy?'

'Because these are the arrangements. You asked to see someone from the *Rezidentura*.'

Lamprecht cradled the 'phone, sitting on the edge of the unmade bed. His suspicions were partly subsiding. The Post Office Directory listed the official occupants of number sixteen Kensington Palace Gardens as the three Soviet service attachés. The K.G.B. *Rezidentura* was hardly likely to be mentioned but the location seemed obvious. Belief nudged his last doubt overboard. Butov outranked the lot of them and it was inconceivable that he would not have been told of such an important defection.

He used the 'phone again, this time asking for a hire-car. There could be no gambling with taxis. Preciseness of timing was important.

'In twenty minutes' time.'

His Tartar face narrowed, hearing the woman's question. 'Where am I going? I shall give the driver instructions when he arrives.'

He watched from the window till a Daimler limousine drew up outside. Its paintwork was leathered to glossy perfection. A man wearing a chauffeur's cap, black tie and blue nylon shirt mounted the steps. Lamprecht threw some money on the table and carried the airline bag downstairs. The woman who had booked him in was waiting in the hallway with the chauffeur. Lamprecht paid for his 'phone calls and breakfast, ignoring the woman's curious looks. He was half way down the steps when someone came running after him. It was the Sinhalese girl, holding out the toothbrush and razor he had left behind.

He stuffed them in his jacket pocket and took his seat in the limousine. Pain surged over his left eye and he bent quickly, covering his face with his hands. The driver's solicitous voice seemed to come through a great rush of falling water.

'Are you all right, sir?'

Lamprecht forced himself to look up into the round ruddy face. 'Quite all right, thank you. I want to go to number sixteen Kensington Palace Gardens, please.'

The momentary pain had been acute yet each attack left his brain clearer, like the flare of a candle before it dies. He sat with the canvas bag nestling between his legs, his eyes on the trees and grass beyond the park railings. The gift of life was so easy to destroy, a simple twist of a switch then annihilation. His death would sadden Barbara but no one else and pretty soon he would be forgotten. The flowers and sunshine would continue as though he had never existed. His left eye was blinking rapidly but the pain had completely gone.

The Daimler swung left, its passage blocked by a red-and-white barrier that protected the entrance. A painted board hung between the twin gates.

Kensington Palace Gardens and Palace Green
NO ADMITTANCE FOR ANY VEHICLES
unless on business in roadway
SPEED LIMIT 20 M.P.H.
By order Crown Estate Commissioners

A gatekeeper wearing a gold-banded top-hat emerged from a booth behind the railings. The chauffeur answered his query confidently.

'The gennelman's going to number sixteen.'

The gatekeeper waddled forward importantly. Lamprecht lifted his head, speaking with authority.

'I have an appointment.'

The barrier was raised, letting the limousine through. Sunshine dappled the ground, filtering through the towering plane trees that extended their boughs across the wide avenue. They drove on slowly, past luxurious and vaguely Italianate mansions that had been built for Victorian millionaires. Only three of the forty-odd houses remained in private hands, the others were diplomatic offices and residences, massive buildings with driveways crowded with cars bearing C.D. plates. It was a world apart, a place of privilege and protocol where each flying standard indicated absolute sovereignty. British authority was limited to the roadway itself. Once beyond the impressive entrances the police had no jurisdiction. There was a second booth a couple of hundred yards away, at the top of the long slope that led down to Kensington. Lamprecht had passed it twice, once in daylight and once at dusk. Glass windows and a rearview mirror mounted outside allowed the uniformed policeman stationed inside a full field of vision. Special Service units patrolled the area and the man in the booth had a hot line to the panic desk at New Scotland Yard. His function was to report any sign of interference with the embassies, demonstrations or picketing.

A single car was parked half-way between the police observation-post and the gloomy ivy-coloured pile of the Soviet Embassy. The fishbowl lamps in the forecourt were still burning. The hire-car chauffeur stopped the limousine in front of an ugly four-storey building. The side door and garage were painted black; a television camera covered the flight of steps leading up to the entrance. Radio aerials sprouted from the flat roof and all the front windows were shuttered. One of the gates was padlocked. The chauffeur turned, his expression doubtful.

'You sure it wasn't number eighteen, sir? This place doesn't look as if anyone lives there.'

Lamprecht leaned forward, offering the man a ten-pound note. 'Thanks for the drive. I won't be needing you any more.'

He was out of the car quickly. As he stepped forward, clutching the canvas bag, a figure appeared in the driver's rearview mirror, the figure of a redheaded woman starting to run. He sprinted into the driveway, hugging the bag to his chest. The door opened at the top of the steps as he neared, allowing him into the dim hallway. He heard the sound of the Daimler pulling away but there were no running footsteps. Sitnikov shut the door and electrically-operated bolts slid into position. Lamprecht wet his lips. The only sound now was the ticking of the clock on the wall in front of him.

Sitnikov was wearing the same Savile Row suit and handmade shoes and a metal badge of some kind stuck in the lapel of his jacket. A broad smile extended on his face as his Baltic-blue eyes settled on the bag Lamprecht was carrying.

'So. You are punctual. Good. Everything is in readiness.'

Stencilled signs in Russian pointed the way up the elaborate staircase. Paint was flaking on the pre-Raphaelite mural and the vaulted ceiling was dusty. Sitnikov turned a handle.

He used the Polish form of address. 'Come in, come in, Pan Henryk.' He stood to one side like a head waiter, allowing Lamprecht to precede him.

The cork-lined door swung on oiled hinges. The vast shuttered room was at the front of the house, the light furnished by an old-fashioned chandelier. There was a Persian carpet but little furniture. Metal files extended as far as an inner door. There was a desk, two chairs, a youthful portrait of Lenin. Beneath it were two men in dark clothing with stubbled heads and anonymous watchful faces.

Lamprecht put the bag down carefully. The door to the hallway was apparently self-locking. He ignored the two men pointedly, speaking to Sitnikov.

'We made an arrangement.'

Sitnikov moved his head from side to side, clucking tolerantly. 'Of course. But first there are things that must be done. You, I am sure, know all about security. Have the kindness please to empty your pockets on the desk.'

The atmosphere was strangely polite, like that of a dentist's waiting room when strangers met. Sitnikov lolled back against the edge of the desk, his hands behind him. His grin widened as Lamprecht added the razor and tooth-brush to the rest of his possessions. Sitnikov flipped through the pages of Lamprecht's passport, inspected the picture of his wife and daughter.

'You travel well-prepared, Uncle.'

'I am a prudent man,' replied Lamprecht. His stomach belied the boast. He hadn't seen who had been in the car with Barbara but there was no indication of pursuit.

Sitnikov nodded approval. 'An excellent attribute. Now I must ask you to take off your clothes.'

Guns leaped in the hands of the guards, the two men misinterpreting Lamprecht's gesture of disbelief.

'The rules are there for all of us,' said Sitnikov.

Lamprecht stood in his socks and underwear as the guards searched his body and clothing thoroughly. Sitnikov slid from the edge of the desk. He was unexpectedly cheerful, helping Lamprecht into his jacket, returning his belongings. He placed the airline bag on the desk.

Lamprecht's warning was quiet. 'Please. The machine is delicate.' Sitnikov thumbed a button on the desk. The door to the hallway opened. He motioned the two guards out. When the door had shut his face was unsmiling.

'Let us understand one another, Pan Henryk. You are selling this machine for money?'

Lamprecht had the impression that everything said was being recorded. 'Half-a-million Swiss francs.'

Green flecks danced in Sitnikov's blue eyes like the patterns in an old-fashioned paperweight.

'And you are ready to demonstrate?'

'Of course.'

There was no noise from outside. It was as if the world had shrunk to the dimensions of this one room. Sitnikov's voice was suddenly edged with sarcasm.

'You are not concerned that we might trick you – that we take this machine and give you nothing? Our experts can solve its secrets, you know. Your position is weak, my friend.'

Lamprecht shook his head. Instinct told him that the end was near. Triumph sang in his brain. Sitnikov's flexing of muscles was typical. The Russians hated an admission of inferiority, even implicit.

'I have worked in Paris as well as in London. You cannot afford to dispense with my expertise. You will keep your promises if only because you need me further.'

Sitnikov clapped his hands in delight, plums of flesh hiding his eyes as he grinned.

'Bravo, bravo! You are an astute man, Pan Henryk. Now there is someone I want you to meet.' He opened the door behind him.

Lamprecht's knowledge of Butov's appearance was based on hearsay and photographs. Rumour had it that the Russian had contracted cancer of the throat though the last picture Lamprecht had seen showed no sign of it. Stolen from a security file in West Berlin the snapshot showed a man in his fifties buying fruit in a Moroccan souk, poised with the coiled menace of a hamadryad, his eyes screwed tight against the glare of the sun. He came through the doorway now, like a cat walking across a puddled barnyard. He was dressed in an open-necked blue shirt with baggy Russian trousers and sandals. His face, arms and chest were deeply suntanned and his white hair lay in fleecy ringlets. His eyes were his dominant feature, cobalt blue with the directness of a laser beam. He moved them from Sitnikov to Lamprecht. There was a leather-padded collar around his neck with a wire attached. The other end of the wire was hidden in the breast-pocket of his shirt. His lips moved without sound, the words coming from the speaker in his pocket instead of his useless voicebox. The effect was like the croaking of a frog.

'Greetings, my friend. I happy to meet you.'

Lamprecht could see into the room behind Butov. The narrow iron-framed bed was covered with a Georgian goathair rug. A holstered pistol hung from the back of a chair. There was a carton of yoghurt on top of some newspapers.

The Pole nodded formally. 'Henryk Lamprecht.'

'Yes,' said Butov, sucking in air and reproducing the words. 'You have changed your name since I last had news of you.'

The words dropped like molten lead into Lamprecht's brain. He dug his fingernails deep in his palms.

'I do not understand.'

Butov's blue eyes pinned him like a butterfly on a board. 'Come now, Pan Henryk. What do you think we are doing in Moscow?'

Sitnikov took it up. 'Do you take us for fools? You left your fingerprints on a glass in that wine bar last night. The characteristics were telexed to Moscow.'

Butov's laugh was a guttural heaving. He moved a chair in Lamprecht's direction, shifting the decoding machine so that he could see the Pole's face.

'Sit, my friend,' he invited. 'And let us talk.'

Lamprecht continued to stand, his back against a filing-cabinet. Sitnikov yawned, shaking his head as if to clear it.

'At the end of the road one rests,' he said.

Butov adjusted the volume of the speaker in his shirt pocket. 'It is a long time since Budapest. I have often thought about you, my friend. I heard that you were dead. I am delighted to see that the report is untrue. You know who I am, of course.' His smile was brilliant.

Lamprecht swallowed the bolt of bitterness. His only hope was to bluff, to continue to lie within the framework of what they already knew.

'Yes. I know who you are.'

Butov looked at square fingernails for a moment. His eyes lifted. 'And why have you come here to see me?'

Silence waited for Lamprecht's halting answer. 'I have often thought about you too. You murdered my wife and child. When I broke the code at the Centre it seemed like a message from the grave, a chance to destroy you.'

A flutter of curiosity changed Butov's expression. 'Destroy me how?'

Lamprecht shrugged. Sweat was dripping from his armpits to his ribcage.

'With the money you pay me. It was about to be arranged. There are people ready to kill if the price is right.'

Butov shook his head, eyes suffused with merriment. 'You are a romantic, Pan Henryk. I give you money to have myself killed? Come now, can that be the truth?'

'You know nothing of hatred,' said Lamprecht.

'True,' agreed Butov. 'Of personal hatred nothing. What happened is twenty years ago and more. And you risk your own life after all this time, for reasons of vengeance? Incredible.'

'Can you think of a better reason?' asked Lamprecht.

Butov explored the back of an ear with a finger. The effort involved in communication seemed to distress him physically. A Y-shaped vein was prominent in his forehead.

'And now, my friend, what now? You seem to have burned your bridges.'

Lamprecht shrugged. People like Butov were used to information that was deviously obtained. They tended to mistrust all else, believing what they discovered unethically.

'I am gambling that you let me live. That you will not provoke a diplomatic incident. It is only five years since the British threw out over a hundred of you.'

'Shit!' said Sitnikov. 'Nobody knows that you are here. The fact that this is with us proves it.' He tapped the canvas bag with manicured fingers.

Butov shifted his chair nearer the inner door, his gaze on the holstered pistol hanging from the chair. He turned to Lamprecht and winked.

'Suppose we arrive at a compromise. We give you your money and pick your brains, the exchange to be made on some neutral soil with neither trusting the other. Come now, think about it. You are no hero, Pan Henryk. There is much in life for you to live for.'

Sitnikov interrupted. 'How long do we have before the loss of this machine is discovered? It is too late to lie. We need the truth.'

The blinding pain was back, twisting Lamprecht's brain inside out.

'Thirty-six hours.' His eyes sought the bag. The chance to trip the hidden switch continued with every second gained. 'But I'd never get out of the country with it.'

Butov reached across the desk and took the machine from the bag. The Cyrillic keyboard winked in the light of the chandelier.

'We can take care of that. I believe you have your passport with you. We can take you directly from here to the airport. A situation to exercise our analytical minds.'

He lifted the decoding machine in a bearlike hug and took it into the adjoining room. Sitnikov followed as far as the doorway, his back to Lamprecht. A couple of seconds passed then the room exploded. Sitnikov's body rose and fell, his legs shorn off at the knees, the flesh spurting blood. The force of the blast ripped through the outer room blowing the desk clean through one of the shuttered windows. The row of metal filing cabinets disappeared as the ceiling collapsed. Sitnikov's truncated corpse lay in what remained of the doorway, still pumping bright arterial blood over the rubble. A length of iron bedstead impaled Butov's body.

Lamprecht staggered through the dense cloud of plaster, his nose and lungs filled with acrid dust. He moved sideways like a crab, choking and dragging the right side of his body. He had no sense of pain at all, little feeling of any kind. He pushed through the jagged window frame and let himself fall to the ground outside. He pulled himself up, propelling himself on knees and elbows laboriously. Blindly he saw the car outside the entrance gate, the rear door open. He lurched towards it, half-deafened eardrums invaded by the jangle of an alarm bell somewhere behind him in the house. He was conscious of helping hands, dragging him into the car and suddenly the noise was gone.

He opened his eyes. The sun was reflected from the blue-black surface of the Baltic Sea. He was in his room in the pine-built summer-house on the edge of the forest. He could hear his mother scolding a maid in the kitchen, the wash of the water on the white sand beach, the bellowing of oxen. Pretty soon he would be as big as his cousins, allowed to ride his father's horse and stay up late for the evening meal. The brilliant light faded quickly into night and he watched the reflection grow on the ceiling as his mother carried the candle upstairs. He smiled as she bent, placing her lips on his forehead. Then he made the sign of the cross and slept.

CHAPTER FOURTEEN

Raven and Zaleski, Slade and McNulty

It was almost nine-thirty when Raven walked onto the used-car lot beneath the Hammersmith flyover. The shops between the arches were devoted to the motor trade, paint-shops, tune-up clinics and cut-price tyre outlets. He made his way through the gate and picked over rubbish towards the shed that served as office. An evil-looking police dog flew at him as he neared, barefanged and snarling. A length of chain attached to a choke-collar brought the beast to a standstill. There was barely enough room for Raven to step by in safety.

The man in the hut removed his feet from a kitchen table, spitting out a mouthful of tea in his surprise. He had the narrow head and the eyes of a collie and a bright red nose. His hair was cut in the style of the forties and he was wearing drainpipe trousers. He put the teacup down and placed his hands on his knees, wagging his head from side to side.

'Well here's a turn-up for the book! If it ain't Sherlock Holmes himself! And what delightful occasion brings you my way, Inspector?'

Raven lowered himself cautiously onto the broken-backed chair. The cracks in the naked floorboards were caulked with scraps of paper and cigarette butts. There was a telephone and an alarm clock on the table, a ring for boiling water and a stained metal teapot. Flies were buzzing around the remains of a corned beef sandwich. The walls were covered with pictures of the royal family and an array of ignition keys hung from hooks on the wall.

A few years before Cherrynose Capstick had been a run-of-the-mill pickpocket with a record of frequent arrests and few successes. A chance excursion to an agricultural fair changed his outlook overnight. Emboldened by draughts of strong local ale he invaded the judges' tribune, leaving it with a wallet containing riches the like of which he had only dreamed. Seven hundred and forty-two pounds cash money had turned him into a staunch supporter of the establishment, a position he protected prudently by supplying the police with occasional snippets of information.

'I want to borrow a car,' said Raven.

Cherrynose flinched as though he had been struck. He combed fingers through the greasy ducktails behind his ears.

'*Borrow?* Nobody makes a living that way, mate.'

Raven took a couple of five-pound notes from his pocket and threw them on the table.

'Just for a couple of hours. You'll have it back this evening at the very latest.'

Cherrynose weighted the two notes with the teapot, his narrow face thoughtful.

'What are you up to these days then? I heard you'd turned a bit dodgy since you left the force. But you always were dodgy so I don't see what difference that makes.'

'You hear a lot of things,' said Raven. He scratched

his ankle above the canvas trim on his sneaker. The gnat bites were still bothering him. 'For instance, I heard that you got rid of some French francs recently. All of it in hundreds. But that's none of my business. Not any more. Know what I mean, Cherrynose?'

'I know,' Cherrynose said morosely. He sniffed hard and rapped furiously on the windowpane. 'That fucking dog's more trouble than he's worth. He don't even know the difference between a customer and these bleeding teenagers we got round here. The buggers'll thieve anything. Know what they did last week? Only fed the dog a couple of pounds of liver, jacked up a Jaguar and rolled the wheels through the front gate. It ain't like when we was kids. There's no respect. What kind of motor did you have in mind?'

Raven leaned back, waving at the rows of ignition keys. The licence-plate numbers were inscribed on plastic discs.

'I'll leave it to you. Something respectable-looking. And I'll want some of your light literature.'

'Light literature?' Cherrynose's face was blank. 'What are you supposed to be talking about?'

'The stickers,' said Raven. Cherrynose's honesty was incomplete. For the right sort of reward cars were left with the keys in them on the lot, to be used on criminal forays and their loss reported at some prearranged time. And hidden on the lot somewhere was a line in windscreen stickers that identified the drivers as Members of Parliament, doctors on call and the like.

Cherrynose reached over Raven's shoulder, smelling of corned beef and hair oil. He plucked a set of keys from a hook.

'This ought to do you, a seventy-four Rover. A beautiful engine, good as new. Belonged to a schoolteacher.'

'I'm borrowing not buying,' said Raven. He lowered his tilted chair to the floor. 'Let's have a look at it.'

Cherrynose opened the door, menacing the police dog with a tyre iron.

'Watch the sod as you go by. Got the postman by the arse a couple of days ago.'

The black car was in the middle lane. There was fuel in the tank and the engine fired first time. Raven nodded. 'It'll do.'

Cherrynose wiped a wing with his sleeve, shaking his head admiringly.

'Listen to that, like a sewing machine. I've a good mind to keep it myself. It'll cost you another ten and I'll throw the paper in for nothing. Want an Old Bill sticker, do you?' The thought of Raven masquerading as a cop sent him into near-hysteria.

Raven handed over the money. 'Press. And make it snappy. I'm in a hurry.'

Cherrynose vanished behind a row of cannibalized vehicles, returning with a piece of rolled-up paper. He watched Raven gum it to the inside of the windshield.

'If it's not back by five o'clock I'll be on the blower to the local nick.'

Raven raced the engine. 'I doubt it.'

Cherrynose leaned against the wing he had just been polishing. 'You're a funny sort of geezer, Raven. I don't know whether I'm doing right.'

'Who does?' asked Raven. 'Get yourself out of the way or I'll flatten you.'

Cherrynose leaped to one side, the echo of his shout dying in the vaulted arches.

'Five o'clock, don't forget!'

Barbara and Zaleski were waiting behind the steamed

windows of the corner café. Raven touched the horn. They hurried out, the girl climbing in behind, Zaleski taking the passenger seat next to Raven. The Pole was strangely thoughtful. Raven turned his head.

'You're sure you still have your B.B.C. pass?'

She opened her handbag, looked inside and nodded. 'Then listen,' he said. 'If we're stopped for any reason by the police you say you're on that assignment, right?'

She combed her long red hair back nervously. 'You mean the programme I researched, the one about Kensington Palace Gardens?'

'Yes. You're still researching it.' He pushed a finger sideways at Zaleski. 'And no pearls of wisdom from you. You're just a friend along for the ride.'

Zaleski pushed away the offending finger with some dignity. 'I am fifty-six years old, mate, and doing this kind of thing when you are in kindergarten.'

A lot had happened and Raven's nerves were raw. 'In Cairo, no doubt,' he said sarcastically.

Zaleski's slate-coloured eyes were quite steady. 'In Cairo. Intelligence Corps, Fifth bloody Polish army, so watch it!'

Barbara slammed the back of Raven's seat with her hands, her voice shaking.

'For God's sake stop this bickering! Or just let me go by myself!'

Raven restarted the engine, shaking his head as he looked at the Pole. 'There's no way anyone can win with you, is there?'

'No way,' Zaleski agreed. 'So drive, inspector-detective.'

Their route took them east into the early morning rush along Kensington High Street. They approached Kensington Palace Gardens from the lower end. The barrier was raised, the scene ahead innocent. The only car in sight was a crashed Porsche in front of the Kuwaiti Embassy. Tourists slung with picnic-boxes and cameras were crowding into Kensington Gardens. Raven drove on, observing the twenty-miles-an-hour speed limit. A uniformed policeman in the observation-post glanced up as they passed. Raven stopped fifty yards on. He could just about read the number on the gateposts ahead. Ivy-covered buildings stretched back from the bosky avenue. A gardener was spraying rose bushes.

'That's the embassy, isn't it?'

Barbara was leaning forward, her bare arms on the back of his seat touching his neck.

'Eighteen is. Sixteen is the office of the service attachés.'

The windows of the gloomy pile were shuttered. One of the entrance gates was closed and padlocked. The house looked forlorn and deserted. Zaleski muttered something in Polish and pointed at the television scanner that angled the top of the entrance steps.

'In Russia we are prisoners. Here they do as they like. Incredible.'

A figure loomed in the rearview mirror, making its way casually towards them. Raven slid into the pose of a man who has nothing to fear.

'Don't look round but there's a cop coming. Relax and try to be natural.'

Zaleski stuffed a cigarette into his holder hurriedly and folded his arms across his chest. The young policeman crossed the roadway, appraising the car and its occupants. Raven turned his welcoming smile round. The policeman leaned both hands on the roof of the car and stuck his head through the open window. His breath smelled of peppermint.

'Good morning. I take it that you people have business in the Gardens?'

Zaleski released a dribble of smoke from the extreme corner of his mouth and tapped ash into the tray in front of him. It was the gesture of an amateur actor demonstrating confidence. The cop's glance settled on Barbara and he saluted.

'Morning, miss.'

The pencil and pad on her knee had appeared from nowhere. She looked up blankly, her face criss-crossed with frown-marks.

'I'm sorry?'

It was beautifully done and Raven wanted to take off his hat to her.

'B.B.C.,' Raven said to the cop. 'Better show the officer your pass,' he added to Barbara.

She hesitated as though dragging her mind back from an intellectual height unknown to them.

'Oh sure. Of course.'

She produced the pass from her bag and held it out for the policeman's inspection. He shifted stance, his manner suddenly confidential.

'You'd think they'd tell us when you people are coming but they don't. We get all sorts up here, all the cranks. Jesus freaks, people who want to get Aunt Hetty out of Russia into Israel, the lot. We had a woman chain herself to the railings a couple of months ago. Outside the French Embassy, banging on about de Gaulle she was and you know how long *he's* been dead! We had to get the fire brigade to cut her free.'

It was ten thirty-five by the clock on the dashboard. 'We're harmless,' smiled Raven.

The cop was disposed to chat. 'I don't watch much telly

myself. You know, weather like this. What do you do then, some kind of chat programme?'

Barbara suspended her scribbling. 'No. It's B.B.C. 2. We're doing a sort of history of Kensington Palace Gardens. I'd recommend it as a nightcap.'

'We do the work and she gets the money,' quipped Raven. Zaleski's belly bulged out over his belt as he inflated his chest and stared loftily through the windscreen. The cop pushed off the roof of the car.

'There you go, there's no justice. Ah well, mustn't waste time fraternizing with the public.' He winked at Barbara. 'Keep your eye on those Arabs, miss.'

'Good girl,' Raven said quietly as he walked away. 'It's only a matter of waiting now. He'll be here.'

She made a sudden violent movement that sent her hair swinging. 'If only I understood what's going on. It's like living in some terrible nightmare.'

A smell of newly mown grass drifted into the car. There was sunshine outside, birds and flowers. A pastoral scene in the heart of the city. Yet an invisible pall of menace seemed to hang over the quiet road. It was the moment to tell her the truth. He took her wrist in his fingers.

He felt her pulse race then she pulled away. Her voice was barely audible.

'It's hard to believe.'

'It's true.' He kept his eyes on hers. 'He's suffering from some sort of brain cancer. What's more he *knows* it. That doctor as good as told me.'

Zaleski came out of his moody silence. 'Dying is time for final solutions. He is Polish.' His acceptance was total.

'It's true,' Raven repeated. 'It's his way of paying his debt.'

'*What* goddam debt?' she demanded, trying to blink back her tears and failing. Her voice was bitter. 'And how about me, goddam him!'

It reminded him of something that Cathy once said, about running where no one could follow. He pushed his handkerchief between Barbara's fingers.

'He loves you and you're expected to understand that. What he's doing has nothing to do with love. It's a matter of retribution.'

Zaleski shrugged, stubbing out his cigarette. 'Is crazy. These savages won't let him past front door.'

'We're going to see that they don't,' said Raven. 'That's why we're here – to stop him.'

'So why waiting?' demanded Zaleski. He pointed up the road like a troop commander leading a cavalry charge. 'Why not going to bloody embassy?'

Barbara pushed the balled wet handkerchief back at Raven. Her face was under control.

'You're his only link with reality,' urged Raven. 'He's not thinking normally. It's up to you, Barbara.'

A removal van passed them and stopped a hundred yards further on. A man in white overalls lowered himself from the cab and went to the back of the van. Raven watched him carefully. The next few minutes would tell if this was some sort of observation vehicle.

He turned his head. The girl's laugh had nothing to do with joy.

'I've never brought luck to anyone,' she announced sombrely. 'Never made a single living soul happy.'

The hint of self-pity grated on Raven. And then he remembered that not so long ago it had been her self-reliance that he found distasteful. He couldn't have it both ways.

'It takes two,' he said. 'One to give and one to take. I've been there. I know.'

She was paying no attention, lost in her own fierce thoughts. 'They're not having him,' she said firmly. 'They are simply not having him!'

A large black Daimler came into view as she spoke. A gambling certainty grew in Raven as the car slowed, made a U-turn and stopped in front of number sixteen. Lamprecht's white head showed as the Pole leaned forward to talk to the driver. The car was no more than thirty yards away. He leaned back and opened the door.

'Don't let him go into that building whatever you do. Tell him we're here to help.'

She was out of the car and running, her voice ahead of her, barefooted and hair and elbows flying. Both men watched as the distance dwindled. But Lamprecht had seen her too and was running, a canvas bag hugged against his chest. Suddenly he was out of sight behind the wall of the Soviet building. Seconds later he appeared at the top of the steps. The front door opened and closed behind him.

Zaleski pulled his head back through the window, his face resigned.

'*A rivederci*, Signor Lamprecht!'

Raven turned on him savagely. 'Open the bloody door!'

Barbara climbed back in as though in a daze and sat with her head hanging. Her arms and legs were shaking violently. Raven's lip had opened again. He wiped his mouth and spat out into the road.

'You did your best.' He could think of nothing else to say.

'*Best?* Why always supposing you know what is best?' Zaleski buttoned his blazer with the air of a man whose advice has been spurned.

'Get out!' flared Raven. 'I don't care where you go as long as it's away from here.'

Zaleski's face reddened but he held his ground. Barbara lifted her head slowly, her cheeks blotched underneath the freckles.

'What did he have in that bag?'

'Guess,' said Raven. 'And I'll pray that you're wrong.'

The removal men up the street were still carrying furniture into a house. Raven's attention was glued to number sixteen. The three of them lapsed into silence, each with his private hopes and fears, unwilling to look at another. Suddenly Raven was conscious of a complete absence of sound as if the whole area was holding its breath. A tremendous clap of thunder followed under the cloudless sky then a deep rumble like an express train speeding through a station. Glass and debris sailed through the foliage, pattering on the roof of the car. Scythed branches swung and then fell.

Raven's hand found the gearshift and rammed it into gear. The car shot forward under a rain of plaster and rubble. The cloud of dust was thinner by the time they reached the forecourt of number sixteen. Lamprecht appeared like a figure in a mirage, stumbling sightlessly, his arms outstretched before him. Great holes gapped the front of the attaché building where once had been window-frames. An alarm-bell was ringing monotonously.

Zaleski burst from the car, his short legs pumping him towards his compatriot. He bent swiftly, picked Lamprecht up in a fireman's lift and staggered back under his load. Barbara already had the rear door open. Together they hauled Lamprecht into the back of the car. Raven swung the Rover in a tight half-circle. The avenue had become bedlam. People were appearing from all directions, the

179

two men from the furniture van running towards them open-mouthed. A front wheel bounced from the kerb. Raven fought the steering. The policeman was out of his booth. He jumped for the pavement as the Rover shot forward. Raven put his foot down hard. A black Mercedes was coming up fast in the rearview mirror, driven from Bayswater Road. He recognized the man at the wheel and his partner. The two cars matched speed, accelerating down the long decline. Raven swung the Rover left at the foot of the slope, veering at the last possible moment. The move scattered pedestrians along the short stretch of roadway. He went right again with the red brick wall a blur on the other side. He could see the Mercedes across the expanse of scorched grass, a couple of hundred yards away and travelling parallel. The arch that rushed at him narrowed to the width of one car. He shot it with no more than inches to spare then wrenched at the wheel, swinging across the oncoming traffic and burning the signals. Horns blared. Shocked faces gaped. A woman shrieked. He barrelled the Rover down a bus-lane, swung left at Queen's Gate Terrace and braked. An outraged matron in a flower-trimmed hat dragged a small dog from under the front wheels. There was no sign of the pursuing Mercedes.

He removed his shaking hands from the steering wheel and twisted in his seat. Lamprecht was lying prone across Barbara Beattie's lap. His clothes were filthy, his jacket ripped at the shoulder seam. There was no blood, no apparent wound but his eyes were closed. Barbara's fingers were stroking the cropped white hair and sallow face.

'We'll have to get him to a doctor. Or rather the other way round. We'll take him to the houseboat and call someone.'

Zaleski spoke with the certainty of experience. 'Is too late for doctor. He is dead.'

Raven grabbed at Lamprecht's limp wrist. It was warm but the pulse was lifeless. The woman on the pavement with the Maltese terrier was staring avidly into the car, her free hand covering her mouth.

Barbara cradled Lamprecht's rolling head against her breast, gazing at Raven with blank bewildered eyes. He wanted to give her his hand. There was nothing else to give except words.

'It's better this way,' he said gently. 'It has to be better, Barbara. He wouldn't have wanted to go on.'

Her voice was as puzzled as her eyes. 'But what *happened* back there?'

He shrugged. 'God only knows. I don't like to think.'

She turned her freckled face away. There was no bitterness in her tone but always the same wonder.

'He died in my arms. I felt him go.'

'Why not?' he asked. Zaleski said nothing. 'Come on,' said Raven. 'We'll go to my place. Whatever has to be done might as well be done from there.' He put the car into gear and they moved forward.

Lights were against them half-way up Notting Hill. McNulty nodded in the direction of the traffic in front of them. It extended for a couple of hundred yards.

'It's worse further up.'

Slade pitched the empty cigarette packet through the open window and opened a fresh one.

'So what the hell are you waiting for?'

The Mercedes was jammed in the outside lane, a taxi in front and a bus behind. McNulty thumbed his horn, signalling his need to pull out. Neither driver gave an inch. He dropped into reverse and crashed the heavy Mercedes against the front of the bus, changed gear and dug his way out of the lane. He covered the distance to the next set of lights driving between the two opposing lines of traffic. The lights changed and he led the charge up the hill. The fury of a hundred horns followed. His grin was exultant.

'That'll teach the fuckers! That's something I always wanted to do!'

Slade fastened his seatbelt. They were travelling at fifty miles an hour on the wrong side of the road. They flashed through four sets of lights at Notting Hill Gate, leaving a wake of dented bumpers, a capsized cyclist and an overturned fruit stall.

'Turn right here!' warned Slade. He wasn't cut out for this exhibitionism. A red-and-white pole barred their way into Kensington Palace Gardens. He could see the gatekeeper's head through the railings. He must have heard the explosion rip down the avenue at the same time as they did. The sandwich he was eating dropped from his hand and he reached behind for his hat.

'Ram it,' said Slade. The Mercedes shot forward, breaking the barrier like a twig and moving into a hail of falling leaves. A Rover was making a U-turn a hundred-and-fifty yards ahead. 'After 'em,' said Slade.

He grabbed one of the handguns from the glove comparment, leaned out of the window and sighted on the Rover's back wheels. There was no chance of a shot and he pulled his arm back. The explosion had blown great gaps in front of one of the Russian Embassy buildings. Debris littered the forecourt. Men were running out through the front door and down the steps. An alarm bell somewhere was ringing stridently. He hung in his seatbelt, shaking his head.

'Jesus *Christ*!'

The implications hit like blows of a hammer. Each one reiterated the promise of disaster.

'That's it,' he said to himself more than to McNulty who was concentrating on his driving.

There were only three people in the car in front. The ex-cop was at the wheel, the Pole and the girl in the back. There was no sign of Lamprecht who must have died in the explosion.

'There can't be anything left of him,' he said out loud. McNulty's eyes were locked on the Rover. The Mercedes gained ground on the long descent but the Rover changed direction at the last possible moment, snaking left too late for McNulty to follow. The Mercedes bounced off a tree. McNulty's jaw muscles knotted white under his brick-red skin. He snarled as he struggled to restart the stalled motor. Through the barrier he turned left and stopped dead. A bus was up on the pavement, its nose against the park railings. Beyond it was a multiple pile-up. A motor-cycle policeman off his machine was trying to straighten out the mess.

'Chelsea,' ordered Slade. 'Make for that bloody house-boat!'

McNulty reversed and joined the westbound traffic. Slade put the gun back in the glove compartment. The radiophone had been switched off since they had left the house on the river. In any case they'd know at the Park all too soon. They'd be out splashing paint over the cracks, covering up any evidence that would involve the Department in the death of a foreign diplomat. Especially a Soviet diplomat. Lamprecht's disappearance in the explosion would make things easier all round. Nobody would ever have heard of this obscure Pole with a grudge. Inside the Department it would be different. Heads would roll. There'd be no paint and no cover-up. Excuse for failure was inadmissible.

They were south of Fulham Road and nearing the river. McNulty slowed fractionally, keeping one hand on the steering wheel and groping for Slade's cigarettes with the other.

'It's a bleedin' bad habit but I feel like one.'

Slade's mind was on other matters. 'Next on your right!'

McNulty spun the wheel with strong wrists and they faced the Embankment. Gulls were circling over the houseboats. The car they were chasing was no more than sixty yards away. Slade had no idea what he was going to say to the occupants. Better in fact to let someone else take the decision. For all he knew, the blanket of silence would cover this trio as well.

'Cut 'em off,' he said curtly.

McNulty obeyed to the letter, swinging the car in a tight circle. An eastbound truck hit them broadside on. The last thing Slade's eyes saw was a gull in the sky.

They watched from the car as the truck hit the Mercedes with all the force of ten tons travelling at forty miles an hour. The overturned vehicle skidded on its roof, struck the stone embankment and stopped with spinning wheels. The truck had stopped a few yards beyond the point of collision, blocking the traffic in both directions. The driver was down from his cab and running across the road. He staggered back, shielding his face from the flames as the fuel-tank exploded in the Mercedes. A factory-whistle blew noon from across the river, the sound launching the gulls from the roofs and rigging on the houseboats. Raven's voice sounded rusty and unused.

'Nobody ought to die like that. Nobody.'

Barbara's freckled face was expressionless. She was still fiercely cradling Lamprecht's head. People were crowding out of the pub. Someone had found a fire extinguisher and was spraying foam on the flames. A police car threaded its way through the stalled vehicles, alarm-signal wailing discordantly.

Zaleski spoke from the back of the car. The tic in his cheek was working overtime.

'Death is always making me nervous. I need a drink.'

'You're an insensitive bastard,' said Raven.

Zaleski shrugged, ignoring the look that was meant to shame him. 'I am East European with varnish of two thousand years' civilization. So death makes me nervous and I drink.'

A cop was running across to the Rover. Others were coming from a second patrol car. Barbara's eyes were still blank. She made no move to take the hand that Raven offered again. The first cop checked the Rover's number plates against a piece of paper in his hand. His jaws slackened as he saw Lamprecht's huddled body. A look of indignation spread across his face.

'What's going on here? Out, *you*!'

Raven pulled the door-catch back. The windows on *Albatross* had been left open and it might be some time before he was back. Blue uniforms crowded in from all sides as his sneakers touched the pavement. Police were trying to force open the doors of the burnt-out Mercedes. A fire-engine sounded in the distance.

Raven leaned forward as the man rummaged through his jeans. Barbara lowered Lamprecht's head to her lap very tenderly. His dead mouth and eyes were half-open. She stared at the cop searching Raven, her face hostile.

'If you're thinking of asking me questions forget it! I'm going to drive this car away and nobody's stopping me.'

A policeman on the other side reached across and plucked the ignition keys from the dash.

'I'd start thinking of the answers if I was you,' he suggested shortly.

Raven straightened his body. 'She'll tell the truth. We'll *all* tell the truth. And no matter what it sounds like it'll still *be* the truth.'

He knew that the smile would be wasted but he offered it just the same.

››› If you've enjoyed this book and would like to discover more great vintage crime and thriller titles, as well as the most exciting crime and thriller authors writing today, visit: ›››

The Murder Room
Where Criminal Minds Meet

themurderroom.com